Jedidiah

KATHI S. BARTON

World Castle Publishing, LLC
Pensacola, Florida

Hardback ISBN: 9781629893556
Print ISBN: 9781629893563
eBook ISBN: 978162989570
First Edition World Castle Publishing, LLC, November 2, 2015
http://www.worldcastlepublishing.com

Licensing Notes

Cover: Karen Fuller
Photographer: Xie4to-graphy
Model: Brian Lewis
Editor: Eric Johnston
Editor: Maxine Bringenberg

Prologue

Eve moved back and forth between the small room and the larger one where her children lay nestled in their protective shells. The kingdom was being ripped apart; her mate, father to her children, was being murdered even as she made preparations for the children she'd never see born. Making one more trip, the one that would give them the key to get to what she had worked so hard to make sure they had, Eve lay down and spoke to her sons.

"You will each, someday, come to be in love. It is the most wondrous feeling of all you will ever feel. If only I could see you then…the grown men that you will be, with the loves of your lives with you carrying on our names and the dragon line. And sons of my good friend Sally…she will help you in ways that I could never do. If only…."

Shifting into a more comfortable position, her heart nearly as dead as her body, she touched her fingers to each of them, then picked up her second born. He was meant for things that would bring much to others…happiness mostly, but some sadness too. But he would be great in his life, bringing magic to those that he loved. Touching her fingers over the crown of his shell, Eve smiled.

"Zak, you will love like none other. Your mate will come to you terrified and full of hate. Not of you but of another, one you will see die by the hand of another, but she will need you no less for it. You and your other half will bring her to love you back." Setting him down, Eve spoke to the others before laying her head down on the warmed stone.

"When I was born, so many centuries ago that I have long since forgotten the year, there were so many of us. Dragons were plentiful, mates and families grew, and more came yearly. Then one year in my youth, a woman—a witch—came to us, warning us all that things were going to change. That soon, all of us would be killed by men, humans. Caroline was not just correct in her telling, but she even went with us when we traveled." She put her hand around Kiaran and held him to her as she spoke. "No one believed her but my father. He packed us up that night, and we left as the skies were turning pink for the new day. As we flew away, another family, this one of greater magic than ours, came with us. That was the family of your grandparents, the sire of your father and his mate."

Her body was dying, slowly but without pain now. As she lay there thinking of them still, her family and how much they had endured to keep her safe, she thought of the couple who would care for her children, Sally and Jacob.

"I knew her family long ago. And that of Jacob. His family was a part of the humans that we had lived with, as was hers. Sally you will come to love as a mother, for which I should be jealous of her but am not. Her grandmother, like her granddaughter, was one of the kindest women I ever met, human or otherwise. She would bring me sweets when she had any to spare, and I would, in kind, take her meat when I was out hunting. It was fair trade for what we gave to each other. Her granddaughter is no different in her love and understanding of us dragons." Closing her eyes, Eve felt Anthony's pain and his urgency to have the young couple understand what he needed from them. "He is a good and wonderful man, your father. So much like his own sire that it takes my breath away to know that he is all mine."

She looked at her children, and then at Zak. Smiling, she touched him again, giving him a little more than she had the rest. "You will survive more than most. Love harder than anyone, and be hurt for it in a way that no one will ever be able to see. Zak, my second born, child of my heart, I will give you a gift. A gift that only a woman of your heart will understand and be able to touch. You will have a child like none other. A child born of magic from all dragons."

Touching him now, she knew that she had only moments to live. Tears burned her cheeks as she thought of all that she would miss. Holding Kiaran to her heart, her body slipped away into death, and she knew. Her last thoughts were that her children would be safe.

Just before her last breath left her body, her heart burned in pain. Not because of the arrow that had pierced it, but because her one and only love was dead as well. Anthony had protected them with all that he had, and she was more in love with him then than she'd thought possible.

"Anthony, my love. I will miss you. Until we are together again." Eve let her body go. Her heart stopped beating, and she did not move again. It was done. Everything was set, and she was done.

Chapter 1

Casdon took to the skies almost as soon as he was released from Elam. He needed this more than he could have told them. To be free of it all, the noise, the people…just to be free. Casdon knew that they wanted him to stay, to have dinner with them, but this was much more important than any food he could consume. The chance to take to the skies.

He never strayed far from the property. To do so would bring unwanted people to their land and so many questions that he was pretty sure no one had the answers to. He didn't even know most of what was going on. And some of it—well, a great deal of it—he just didn't care about. Living here, with the family, was wonderful to a point, but he missed the quiet when it had been just him and Elam in his home.

Landing at the top of the biggest mountain, he watched the movement below him. Deer played in the field, as did other animals, some of them too small for him to make out at this great distance. But it was peaceful here, a place that he came to more often than not just to simply enjoy himself.

Lying down, he watched the deer eating, and when his belly rumbled in hunger he thought seriously about going home, but he stayed if for no other reason than he was simply too relaxed to get up. But when the deer scattered, he sat up and watched carefully for what might have disturbed them. When he saw the man, boy really, Casdon lifted his body from the ground and took to the skies to teach the child a lesson on being where he was not invited.

When the being moved deeper into the trees, Casdon lost sight of him. Shifting from dragon to man, he moved quietly through the woods until he had his scent. The smell of rotted meat made him sneeze, and he heard someone laughing deeper into the woods from where he stood. Moving now, thinking of all the things he was going to do to the man, he was hit from behind, his body falling hard to the ground.

The body atop his was slight. Casdon knew that he could have gotten up, even shifted to show his strength, but he stilled, holding onto his temper as the man held something sharp to his head.

What's the matter? He told Essie that he was fine, just having some fun, but she said she was coming to him.

No. Don't do that. I'm fine. A man has gotten the jump on me because I have allowed it, but I fear that he is ill and I don't want to hurt him. Casdon moved his head slightly to get a look at the man, but the sharpness at his head dug deeper. *If you startle him, he'll remove my head before we can explain anything to him.*

He's going to pay for harming you. Casdon almost laughed at the furiousness of her tone. Essie was his queen for sure, and she took her duty to protect very seriously, but he was a dragon, after all. Then he realized that the man had yet to speak, and he tried again to turn to look at him.

"Are you aware that you are on private land?" Nothing happened, except the sharp point digging into his skin until he felt the droplet of blood race down his neck. "You have drawn first blood. That makes you the victor in our fight. Let me up and I shall give you my hand."

When the weight at his back shifted, so did Casdon, letting his animal take him so that he'd be safe. His dragon felt good after being held captive as he'd been, but he nearly fell back when he looked at the man, who was not a man at all but a woman.

She'd fallen back, her body hitting the ground, and she scrambled back from him. He wasn't sure who of them was more startled, her or him, but she was most assuredly more afraid. When he took a step to her she backed up again, using her elbows and feet to move like a crab across sand. Casdon stopped moving and pulled his wings to his body. The quiver of arrows at her back shook with her fear.

"What are you?" Had she spoken before now, he would have known her gender. Even to have glimpsed her, there would have been no doubt that she was all woman. "I asked you a question. Did he send you here? Are you to take me back to him? I won't go. Not easily I won't."

Casdon couldn't speak to her in this form, but he could hear well. Something…or someone…was crashing through the woods toward them, and when he reached out, he could feel the man's intent, which was to kill the woman…but not before making her suffer a great deal. Moving toward her, his wings spread wide, Casdon snatched her up and into his claws just as the man came near the clearing where they were.

She didn't struggle as he thought she would but held onto his claws as if she were afraid that he'd drop her. He would never do that, but he felt good that she wasn't fighting him. As he flew over the field where they had been, he could see the man and knew that had they not left, he would have harmed them. Casdon took her to his mountain top and put her down before dropping to the ground with her.

"You saved me. Why?" He only stared at her, not sure if he were to shift back to man she wouldn't run again. "Can you be that guy again? Please? I'm freaking out a little."

Doing as she asked, Casdon bowed low and then smiled at her. "This is more to your liking then?"

"Not really, but it's better than thinking that you're going to tear me to pieces before you burn me and have me for dinner." He said nothing as he watched her. "What are you?"

"Dragon, as you can see. And for the record, I don't eat little girls for my dinner. They're better as a snack. Not as much to weigh on my belly before I take on villages and burn them to the ground." He'd meant it as a joke, to make her laugh, but she only stared at him. "I was kidding you. I don't eat humans any more than you do dragons."

"How do you know that I don't have one of you tied up in the barn on my property?" He leaned into her shoulder and sniffed her. When she smacked his nose, he backed up quickly. "Just how rude do you have to be to make the point that you're bigger than me?"

"My size? It bothers you?" She didn't answer him, but she did look down the hillside. When she sat down, he moved to sit by her, but not close enough that she could hit him again. He thought her slightly unbalanced, but he was sure it was from him and not her usual state.

"Men are all pieces of shit, not just you. And their size matters little. Some of the meanest men I know are no bigger than me, but just as mean as a man twice their size." He wanted to ask her why she thought that, but she continued before he could. "Thank you for saving me from him. He'll find me eventually, but right now...well, thank you."

"He is related to you somehow?" Instead of answering him, she stood up and started down the hill. Casdon watched her for a moment before he followed her. He had no idea why he didn't just let her go, but he felt the urge to keep her protected, even if it was from herself.

She moved like she was one with the ground. Her feet didn't seem to stumble on any rocks and she didn't need to catch herself on trees as she moved with greater speed toward the bottom. Casdon had to hold on several times when his body got ahead of his feet, and when he tripped a couple of times, had it not been for the trees near him he would have surely fallen on his head. When they reached the bottom, where the ground was level, she didn't look back but kept going in the opposite direction of where they'd left the man.

"You're not safe out here." He thought she said something like no shit, but he was too busy looking for the man to worry about her insulting him. "There are more of my kind out there too. If you run into any of them, I'd not hit them with my hand; they might remove it for you."

That stopped her, which she did so suddenly he bumped into her and they both fell to the ground. He was hit several times before he was able to get her hands captured in his. Telling her to stop it had no effect on her. But as soon as he had her hands, he looked into her face. She was terrified, more so than when he'd been a dragon.

"I won't hurt you." She tried to buck him off, but he was heavier and stronger than her, and all she managed to do was wear herself out. "Be still for a moment and I'll let you go."

The branch breaking so close to them had him letting her hands go but not allowing her to get up. The man that had been crashing through the woods earlier was standing not ten feet from them, and the gun in his hand looked ready to be used. The girl put her hand over his and held it to her mouth as she screamed behind it. Casdon knew then that whatever the relationship was between the two of them, she was not going back with the man.

"Girl, where the hell are you?" Casdon looked down at her, and her head nodded at his unspoken question. It was her he was looking for. He'd known that, of course, but now it was confirmed. "Lindsey, I'm not going to tell you again to get yourself to me. I've had a bad day and there ain't no reason for you to be acting like this. Get on back to the house and I'll let you have a bone for your supper. Come on now. You've been out here for a week, long enough for to have gotten this crap out of your system. Get yourself here now."

Casdon felt her teeth graze his skin just before she bit into his flesh. It wasn't painful, not really, but he felt her draw on the wound and take his blood into her mouth. As soon as she swallowed, he felt the connection to her immediately.

I'm not his daughter or any relation to him. He uses me for his housekeeper mostly. But I've no desire to go back to him. I won't be chained up like an animal again, and I will not be starved because he has the key to my freedom. And just last week, he…he wanted more than for me to clean his house.

Casdon felt his host call to him. Elam would come to him now because he could feel his fear, but he told him to stay where he was, that he would explain when he found him. To the girl, he asked what the man wanted from her now.

He didn't think she'd answer. There was something so profoundly sad about her. When she shifted a little, he saw that her arrows, a dozen or so of them, were all handmade, and well done too. Casdon wondered where her bow was, and thought perhaps she'd dropped it when he picked her up. Now, he realized, she had no way of protecting herself because of him. The man, he only just realized, was gone now.

Nothing. When she shoved him off, he moved rather than fight with her. The man was close still, but not where they could see him from their position on the ground. And when she moved up to her knees, carefully looking around her before standing, Casdon wondered how long she'd really been hiding from the man. More than the week the man had accused her of, he'd bet.

He didn't go after her when she moved deeper in the woods. By her taking his blood into her body, he had a connection with her now. He knew that should he want to he could find her in the deepest caves, as well as know when she was hurt or sick. Casdon lay there thinking that he'd had the most fun he'd had in a good long time when she came into his life.

Making his way home, he also kept an eye out for the man. Having his scent now too, he knew that as soon as he was home and talked to the rest of them, all of them, he'd be back to find him…and to set him straight on a few things. But the moment he walked in the door, Jed started in on him.

"When we call you, you're to come." Casdon told him that he'd never called him, and he'd been talking to Elam and Essie too. "We did. For over an hour after you talked to Essie. And we were about to go out and find what had befallen you when Elam felt you again. Were you hurt? Have you been in a deep cave?"

"No. I've been walking the woods. There is a man in them that has it in his head to…to shoot our deer." Casdon had no idea why he didn't mention the girl. He'd thought about it when he was walking home, but the moment he stepped in the house, all thoughts of telling his family what he'd seen and done with her went out of his head. For some reason, he wanted to keep her to himself for a time.

Jed watched him, looked at him as if he knew what was going on, but Casdon moved to the stairs and to the room that he shared with Elam and sat on the bed. Elam came in a bit later and asked him if he was all right.

"Yes. Jed said that you'd been trying to reach me. I didn't hear you." He wondered if the girl had done that, but had no way of knowing. She'd taken his blood, but he'd not tasted hers. "I'm sorry to have worried you all unnecessarily."

"I was worried when I hit the wall. All I could think about was that the witch had come back." Casdon nodded but didn't say anything. Elam told him what was said at dinner. "The castle is coming along nicely, and Jed has the plans ready to send to the woodcrafter to start working on the tables and such. It was good that Elbert knew the man that they used as a measuring stick back then."

All the dimensions for the castle and its contents were in a diary that Jed had found a couple of months ago. Most of it was hand-drawn pictures of things, like the wall hangings and portraits. There was a mention of the people who had done the work as well, and what was paid to them for it. One family that they'd read about had gotten ten sheep for their work on the garden, and another family had gotten a home without taxation for the rest of their lives.

Casdon had wondered why everyone wasn't given land to live on, and Caroline, the white witch, had told them that his dad had given to the people what they needed, not what they wanted. Sometimes it was difficult to know what to give, but their father had known. It was what had made him a great king.

Just after nightfall, Casdon went out to the porch to take in the night sounds, and when Essie asked to join him, he moved over on the swing and sat in a comfortable quiet with her for nearly an hour.

"Who is she?" Casdon looked over at her and said nothing for several seconds, hoping he'd heard her wrong. "When I couldn't find you I asked the earth where you were, and it said that you were with a woman and that you were saving her from herself. Is she your mate?"

"No. Not that. Someone is trying to kill her. Well, maybe not kill her, but he will hurt her should he find her. But for now, she's safe I think." Essie nodded. "I don't know what she is or who, other than her first name is Lindsey. She…she bit me when we were being tracked by this man and I could talk to her. I never tasted her."

When Essie spoke again, he knew that she'd found the girl and had asked the earth to protect her. "She's unwell, did you know that? I don't mean just hurt, but sick as well. The earth said that she will need someone to heal her before she can take on the man. He is bent on having her as his bed partner."

"That's kinda what I thought too." Casdon looked out over the night sky and darkness he knew to be the trees. "She's afraid of him. She told me that he used her as a housekeeper. I think she skipped over the part of how long she's been with him. Her fear is not fresh, but resigned somehow. As if she knows that he'll find her again and that she will, in turn, run again."

"No. If he catches her this time, she won't be able to run again." With that she moved into the house and left him there to think and ponder over what she'd said. Going to the lawn, he shifted again and took to the skies. Casdon needed to know where the man was and that the girl was indeed safe. And the only way to do that was to find them.

~~~

Lindsey went deeper into the cave that she'd found earlier that day. Up until a few mornings ago she'd been living in a hut that had been abandoned not long ago. And while it was warm when the fires were burning, it was kind of creepy in what was on the shelves and hanging from the ceiling. Not to mention, the place had smelled badly too. After only about three nights she'd moved on, and had been, until now, living in trees and under piles of leaves. It wasn't a way to live, but she was afraid to go to the town yet. He would find her there for sure.

Brandon Cox had hired her to take care of his home over a year ago. It wasn't like it was yesterday, but
~~~

sometimes she forgot that fifteen months had passed between then and now. She'd told the man that had changed into a dragon that she was his housekeeper because she was embarrassed that she'd not been able to escape before now. Not that she'd not tried, but this time something had happened that had afforded her a better opportunity than the other times.

She was his slave, and if her lack of pay didn't say that, then the fact that he'd chained her to the floor all the time would certainly be good evidence of it. She had wanted out from the very beginning. This was the longest that she'd been away from him, and she was afraid of what he'd do when he found her again.

"I will kill myself." The sound of her voice startled her, and she looked around to make sure that no one had heard her. Lindsey had no idea what was in the cave with her, but if they were to speak to her, she thought that she'd just mark it up to more shit that she didn't know about. And there had been plenty she'd discovered.

The dragon man for one thing. Who the hell would have thought that they were real, much less around her? She'd seen other shifters, mostly wolf and cat, but nothing like a dragon. And he seemed just as comfortable in one body as he was in the other. The others, the other shifters, had seemed like they'd rather be one or the other, not both. At least she had thought so at the time.

When the cave she was in leveled out and it was easier to walk, Lindsey sat down on the ground and couldn't believe how warm it was. She laid her head back on the big stone behind her and thought of a warm fire and a good meal. It had been so long since she'd had either that she feared that cold berries and worm-filled apples were all she was going to get. But someday, she told herself, someday she'd have more than enough food, and warmth so wonderful that she'd never move away from it. Then she thought of the dragon man.

He had saved her not once, but twice today. Most would have just left her to her own problems and not cared a bit for her. It was the way things had been since she could remember…what she could remember, which was very little at all of her time before the home.

But he had helped her get away from Brandon and had kept her from leaping up and running at him when he'd come to the clearing. Biting him had been a mistake, she knew this now, but there wasn't anything she could do about it. Her one friend had told her that they could talk that way. It really was too bad that he'd died some months before she was held captive. It would have been wonderful to have someone to talk to all these past months.

Lying down to a more prone position, Lindsey thought of how handsome the man had been. Not just as a man, which was nice enough, but as his dragon. He was pretty. Wondering if pretty was a word that one used when describing a dragon, she smiled in the darkness. But his dragon self was very handsome. And very strong. Strong enough to lift her up in his claws and take her to safety.

Her belly rumbled in protest of not having anything in it, and she lay there wishing she'd remembered to pick herself an apple or two before coming down here to sleep. The worm holes in them didn't bother her overly much. She was careful not to bite before looking, but that didn't make her any less hungry. Closing her eyes and promising her belly a meal soon, she tried to sleep.

Being hungry and tired was something that wasn't new to her. It depressed her to think how long it had been since she'd been full. And sadder still to know that the only good bath she'd had recently was the dip in the lake she'd found a few days ago.

While the water had been very cold coming from the mountain, she felt wonderful after she'd scrubbed first herself, then her clothing. And when she'd stripped them off, meager as they were, and laid them out to dry, Lindsey had spent a good hour just wading in the clear water, feeling free.

But she'd paid for her time in the water. Time had slipped away from her, and Brandon had nearly caught her. Well, he did find her, but he'd not taken her this time. Moving to look at the tear in her pants, she could see the wound and thought it wasn't healing like it should. Running today had cost her as well, and she'd worn out much sooner than she had when she'd first gotten away.

"He's hit me with that whip for the last time." Looking around when she thought she heard a voice tell her to take her gift, she sat up and tried to see into the darkness. "Who's there?"

There was no answer, but Lindsey had a feeling that she was being watched. Not by anything that would harm her, but watched all the same. Lying back down, she tried to think of something else, a good thought, when the dragon man came to her mind again. He was a nice man. Too nice for the likes of her.

It had taken her nearly all her life to realize that no one was coming for her when she'd been at the home. It had been like she'd woken up there, not that she'd been taken there like the other kids. The memories before that time were blurred. There were images of two men, one of whom she knew by name, and her grandmother. A house and a dark night, but not where it was or why the man had been carrying her.

But in all that time there, years and years, no one had come for her. Not her parents, who she had surmised more than likely didn't care that she was gone, or anyone else, like the grandma that she'd met only a few times. And no matter how hard she'd tried, there was simply no information to be found about them. No one by the name Decker had lost a child. And the police were less than helpful when she'd gone to ask them what they might know.

Brandon was one of them, a cop. So she knew she would get no help from them with keeping him away from her or getting him to leave her alone. After a while she'd given up on everything, like a warm bed and good food, until a few weeks ago.

Brandon had come home when she'd been at her bath. It was nothing more than her standing in the kitchen in a big tub, but he'd caught her naked. She might have run then, but her chains were too tight and he'd hit her and knocked her out when she cringed from him. After that, it was as if he'd been waiting to catch her naked again so he could touch her. And when he did, she felt her skin crawl and her belly sick up.

"You look ready for me to sleep with." He'd told her that when he'd come to her that day. "And if you scream out, I'm going to hit you until you're out. Then I'm going to do it to you some more. You're prime for me, and I should have seen it before now."

He'd unbuckled his pants and pulled out his dick. He was hard but small, and she'd wondered what he thought he was going to do with it. She'd had sex before and knew how it worked, but he was so tiny…like a little boy's thing. But then he came at her, grabbing her by the arm and pulling her down to the floor and near his groin. Lindsey had done the only thing she could think of, and had slammed her fist into his balls and knocked him down.

As he had lain there, bleeding from his head where he'd hit the table, Lindsey tried to think past what had just happened. She thought that he'd wake and hit her harder this time, and make good on his promise to rape her. But then she realized that he was really out, and crawled to him to get the key that was forever hung around his neck. Taking it, she unlocked her chains and ran around the house, looking for things to take with her. There wasn't much, but she did manage to find some things…mostly food and the bow and arrow she'd brought with her the first day.

It had been a gift from her friend, the wolf. He'd even gone so far as to show her how to use it. She wasn't all that good at it, but it had been fun learning. And lately, at least before getting trapped here, she'd been able to hit the tree she'd been aiming at more often than not. But she could never bring herself to kill a bird or anything else to eat. It was just too...mean, she supposed, was a good word for it.

All that she'd been able to carry was one bag that she'd stuffed with things to eat and a knife. The one that was still in her pocket. There was never any water in the house unless she went to the creek to get it, as he wouldn't let her use the sink water. Said it was his and his alone. The moron. How the hell was the water his when he barely even used it to clean himself? Not to mention, he'd worn his clothing for days on end before he'd tell her to wash and dry them. He really was a fucking moron.

Curling into a ball to get warm from the sudden chill, Lindsey fell asleep. Tomorrow was going to be better, she told herself. But then, she told herself that daily and it had yet to happen. But now…well, now she had a little hope. Not much, but enough to put a smile on her face, and she liked it. The smile felt really good for a change.

Chapter 2

Jed pulled his shirt up and over his head and dropped it on the ground. It stank worse than he did, and when he moved it past his nose, he nearly got sick from it. Smiling, he looked over at Zak, his dragon, when he laughed too.

The dragons were doing most of the heavy lifting. He and his brothers were doing a lot, too, but they left most of the largest stones that they were pulling out of the pile of rubble that had once been a thriving castle. And what a pile of stone it was. He supposed he should have known that it was going to be a big undertaking, but seeing it and thinking it were two entirely different things. When Essie brought him a bottle of water he nearly drained it, but she cautioned him about the cold and his being hot.

Taking slow sips, he watched the rest of them. The twelve of them, five his brothers and the six dragons that were their other halves, had been at this for nearly a week. To him it looked as if they'd made little progress, but he knew that wasn't right. The stone had fallen in on the castle, and according to the notes he'd found, there were two levels below the ground that they had to yet get to.

The three levels of it had been above the ground had fallen in, and was what they were currently cleaning up.

So far they had found a few of the items that had been in the castle. One was a large pot. He'd had no idea what it had been used for until they looked in the book. That was what led them to believe they had found part of a bedroom. The chamber pot, it turned out to be, had been in one of the several bedrooms on the upper floors. A part of a blanket, too, had been found. But it was so eaten up by something that they'd put it aside in a bag. But the real treasure had come in the form of a woman's hair comb. No one knew who it had belonged to, the household or their mother, but it, too, was something that they held near to their hearts.

"I've been thinking." Everyone groaned at Casdon. "Seriously. Yesterday I found someone on our land that should not have been here, as I mentioned before. Not just the man—I'm not concerned with him—but there was a woman. I think she needs to be here for our protection, and the man who was after her needs to be taught a lesson. By us. Which reminds me, how are our tenants and where do they stand with living on this land?"

"We have tenants? And what woman? No one said anything about a woman." Jed looked at Asher, who also acted as if he had no idea. They all turned to Elbert when he and Dad came from the woods. "We have tenants on this land?"

"You do. Seven I believe. They are to pay homage to the family once a year, or so I have been led to believe. They are all current but one. And the attorneys are working to have him evicted as we speak. His payments are several years in arrears." Elbert handed Jed a sandwich as he continued. "He is a man that I do believe that Casdon has had dealings with. But like you, I know of no woman."

Jed, as did the rest of them, looked at Casdon. His face was bright with embarrassment, and he smiled lamely at him. He had heard about the man this morning at breakfast, but didn't remember any mention of a woman. Jed asked him now.

"He was after the girl. The one that I just mentioned to you guys." Jed tried to wrap his head around someone chasing a girl on their land. He wasn't stupid…he knew that it sometimes happened. But not on their land. There was magic here to protect all that lived here. But he supposed that if the man lived here too, he was sort of exempt from the magic. He'd have to ask Caroline when he saw her again.

"Do you know where she is now?" Casdon told him. "So, she's living in the caves. And do you know if she has enough to eat? Is she unwell?"

"I'm not stupid, Jed, and I would very much appreciate if it you'd stop talking to me as if I am." Jed snapped his mouth closed. Casdon had been short with them all lately, and they wondered about it. When he said he was sorry, Jed looked at Elam, who only shook his head. "I took her some food this morning before coming here. And water. I'm not sure that she had a coat or anything, so I took her one of mine to wear. Also, I know I should have asked, but she lost her bow yesterday and I don't know if she's found it or not, so I took the one from the storage shed and left that as well."

"Good job." There was the matter of his temper, but Jed would talk to him later, when they were alone. Or have Elam do it. Instead, he continued with what to do about the girl. "We should find her and bring her to the house. If for no other reason than she can't stay out there in the cold. Winter will be here before we know it, and the mountains and the caves will be coldest."

"I've had the earth keep her warm." Essie sat down and looked at them all. "I knew that he'd been with her yesterday. And that was why I wasn't worried when we couldn't find him. The earth told me that he was with her, trying to save her from herself and the man that chased her. She's hurt too. Something to do with an infection, but I can't tell where."

Jed wrapped his sandwich up, as did the rest of them. Break was over for now, and they all moved toward the mountain that Casdon said the girl was at. Essie laughed and said that she'd get a room ready for her and would see them later. Asher was smiling like a loon when he glanced over at Jed.

"You're happy." Asher looked at him and nodded. "It looks very good on you. I was—a little mind you—worried about what was going to happen with the two of you. Kiaran and you were mates to the same person, but I can see that you've made it work out."

"We both love her very much." Jed nodded. "You think we'll all have mates that we share with the dragons? I don't know how it would work otherwise. I mean, I suppose there could be two women for us, but this works for us."

"I don't know how it will work for the rest of us to be honest. Nor, really, do I think it will matter how it works so long as you're all happy." Jed had thought of nothing else in his spare time but having a mate and how much she would change his life. "I'm not saying that I'd rather not have a mate, or even both of us having one each for that matter, but I don't...I'm not sure I could handle one."

"What do you mean 'handle one'? They're not anything that you need to handle, Jed. Essie is amazing." Jed agreed with him and said that he loved her too. "Then I don't understand why you'd think your mate will be different."

"Because it's me." That was a stupid answer, so he tried again. "I mean, I'm not good around the opposite sex. I can't seem to get a word out without pissing them off. It's why I don't date all that much. Women just don't like me. And when I try to be charming, I come off as a weird person and they put restraining orders out on me." It had never happened really, but he'd been warned off a couple of times.

"That's the stupidest thing you've ever said. What about that girl…what was her name?" He told him. "Yeah, Cindy…what about her? You and she had a thing going for a while. How do you think that worked with you two?"

"She was as rude as I was." Jed couldn't help it, he laughed with Asher. "We would be so mean to each other. I'd tell her she was lazy or putting on a few pounds, whatever, and she'd come back at me with this stupid thing about my tat. I never told her about Zak, but I don't think he much cared for her either."

"I didn't care for her at all." Jed patted his counterpart on the back as they climbed the big hill that the cave was in. "When Jed would sleep, she'd try to wipe at me with nail polish remover and all kinds of things. That's what ended the relationship, I think…her trying to make him into something that he wasn't ever going to be. A man without me."

Jed smiled at the memory, and Asher asked what it was. "She tried to get rid of Zak, like he said, and once he'd had enough, he rose up from me and snapped at her. It woke me, of course, and when she went screaming to the bathroom, Zak told me what she'd been doing. Needless to say, once that was out, I moved to my own place. So as you can see, I don't do well with women."

The cave was right in front of them and all the food and stuff that Casdon had brought was still where he'd put it. He looked worried, and that in turn worried them as well. Going into the cave, Asher lit the way for them with his magic, and it wasn't until they came to a few forks in the path that they decided to split up.

Jed and Zak went down and the rest of them went in the other directions to save time. They could communicate if they needed to, but for now, they moved quietly. Jed was sort of afraid to find that the man had found the girl and she was going to be dead. Asher, however, assured them that she was alive but very sick. Zak said that he wasn't sure that was going to be any better.

Zak stopped him nearly at where the path leveled out. They could see that the cave was brighter here. Not by fire, but perhaps because the cave was helping them. As they moved closer, they could just make out a body. As Zak moved to be his dragon, he took off to the topmost part of the cave while Jed moved up behind the body. He saw that she was hurt badly.

Jed reached out to the rest of his brothers to tell him where she was and what was going on. They were on their way.

"She's been beaten pretty badly. Do you have an idea who it might be?" Zak didn't answer him, but then he was being a lookout not there to cool his temper. "I'd like to find the person who did this to her and beat the living snot out of them.

His temper of late had been short. Well, more than that, it had be violent and hot. He wanted to hurt anyone who spoke to him, not caring a fig if it made sense or not. Jed went to the wall and started knocking his head against the hard stone. He needed something to distract him from his anger. He was jerked away suddenly and looked at his older brother, Asher.

"I'm all right now." He wasn't immediately let go, but Jed assured him he wasn't going to hurt anyone. Trying to shake off his anger, he looked at the woman in front of them, laying in the dirt and bleeding from her nose and mouth. "Something happened here and I'm not in the best of humor about it."

"Really? Because here I thought you were getting better all the time." Asher hit him on the shoulder before going to stand over the prone woman. "Christ, you scared the shit out of me. I've never seen you look so murderous before."

"I've never felt that way before." He was still standing there when he felt Zak touch his mind, and he realized that both Zak and the woman were gone. Jed asked him if he'd taken the woman back to the house, and he said that he had.

She's the one, Jed.

Jed was moving toward the opening of the cave with Asher when he realized what Zak had said. He stood there for several seconds, just trying to get his mind to stop for a moment.

Your mate? He told him she was. *And do you think…please tell me you don't think she's mine too.*

I have no way of knowing that until you get here. Jed decided that he was never going home again. *Yeah, that'll work. You moron. Get here so we can figure this out. And so you know, she's got a bad infection on her leg. It looks like someone hit her with a whip and they didn't care how deeply it went.*

"I'm going to kill him."

Asher asked him who, and that was when Jed realized he'd spoken that part out loud. "Jed?"

"I need to go to town for a few days." Zak laughed in his head. "I don't know how long I'll be gone. Maybe I'll not come back."

"She's your mate." Jed nodded at Asher, who then burst out laughing. "Zak told Essie what was going on with him. I'm assuming she's yours too, right?"

"I don't know. I just…I just told you I don't know what to do with a mate. What the hell am I going to do with her?" Asher told him to love her. "I don't know how. I don't even know if I want to know how."

"Then maybe it would be best if you did leave." Asher called to Shane, and they started their walk back to the house. Jed was still standing there when the cave was empty of everyone but him. Sitting down on the cold earth, he tried to think his way out of having a mate. But all he could think about was he had her and that he was so screwed.

~~~

Jacob went from wanting to beat his son to going out and making sure he was all right. It was nearly pitch dark out and no one could get in touch with him. Essie had told him several times that he was still in the area, but Jed had had a powerful awakening today and he might need him. And Jacob wanted this business of him seeing if the young girl was his mate confirmed. He needed to know that the girl was going to be all right now.
~~~

Going back up to the room that Zak and Jed shared, he wasn't surprised to see the dragon, now as a man, there. He was watching over her like she was a treasure. Which, Jacob realized, she was. The fever in her leg was burning her up one minute and having her shaking so badly with the chills the next that he was worried about her breaking bones. She wasn't very big…tall, but no bigger than a slim tree in her weight.

"I've been giving her the broth like Essie said. But I think I spill more of it than I get in her." Jacob nodded and sat on the chair next to the bed. Zak looked worried, and so was Jacob. "Jed said that he's not coming here again. Told me that he doesn't know what to do with her, so he's going to keep away. You think that'll work?"

"No. Do you?" Zak shook his head. "Mayhap she's not his mate too. You ever think of that? She might just be for you?"

"Do you think so?" No, he didn't, and told Zak that. "Me either. But it will do neither of us any good if she doesn't break this fever soon. She's so weak to begin with, and I don't think she's eaten a proper meal in some time."

Jacob could see that too. She looked…sunken, he supposed was a good word for it. Her lips were cracked and peeling, her cheeks were deep crevices in her face that make her appear to be nearer to death than he could bear, and she looked like she'd been wearing the same clothing for some time. Clean, but they were worn almost to nothing but a few threads in a lot of places. When she started shaking again, he looked at Zak.

"When they brought Essie here, Asher climbed into bed with her naked so she'd be warm. I'm not saying you should do that, but it might help keeping her warm when she's shaking like she does." Zak said he'd do that. "And a shower. I'm not sure what that might do for her, but she might feel a bit better cleaned up, and the warm water would make her warmer on the outside too. I know I would."

She wasn't just dirty, but muddy too. While in the cave, Jacob thought perhaps that the dirt had clung to her while she'd been fevering, and when she was chilled it had caked on her as well. He could see that her hair was thick with it, as well as her nails and feet. Poor thing was just covered in it.

The water turned on in the bathroom, and he looked at Zak. The boy had some powers that he didn't brag about to anyone, and he was pretty sure that Jed had no idea what some of them were. Jed, he knew, had a few of his own, more than likely something from being with Zak all this time. Zak's momma had given him a little extra, might even have given them all a little extra, and they knew what they were already. As Zak stood up and started to strip down, Jacob left him to his job. He reached for his son and told him what was going on.

You want her to die, then you go on ahead and keep pouting like you're five or so. Not a man nearly three times the age of most trees. Jed didn't answer him. *Zak is here doing all he can for her, and you're sitting out there with your thumb up your nose and acting like you been hurt. Well, what you gonna do, son, if she dies? Wonder for the rest of your life if she was the one and you flittered it all away?*

I didn't ask for this. Jacob told him no, he'd not done that, but he had it all the same. *What if she hates me?*

Right this minute, I don't like you overly much either. And if you let her die because you're too stupid and stubborn to get your butt in here and see to her, then I'll never forgive you for this, Jedidiah. Sure as I'm standing here as your daddy, I won't. There isn't no reason for you to let her go just because you think you might not want her. How is that fair to that poor thing up there, I ask you?

He heard the door open downstairs and then the steps creaking. When Jed was standing in front of him, Jacob wanted to first hit him, then hug him hard. Jacob looked at his son and wondered what the hell had gotten into him to make him so stubborn. He didn't get any of that from him. Jacob looked up at his second born and felt his heart twist up for all that the boy had gone through, and how much more he was going to have to endure.

"You did the right thing." Jed nodded and looked at his bedroom door. "Go on in. I'm betting Zak is having a hard time getting her in the shower with him. It's hard to hold onto an unconscious person, I'm betting."

Jacob went down the stairs and out into the yard. He'd made his way to the graves several times over the last few weeks, and headed there now. It bothered him to see his own there, the dates so far gone that he didn't even remember the weather back then. But his wife, his Sally, he did remember the day that she'd passed. With all his heart.

"Jed has him a mate now. I'm not sure how that one is gonna work out, but he's got her. Her name is Lindsey. So I guess so if you got yourself any of the power you had when we were living, I'd like for you to use a little on her. She's really ill and might die. Elbert seems to think she's going to be fine with what they're doing, but I don't know."

Jacob started pulling weeds off her grave and then looked over at his. Last time he was here, he'd put a blanket over it. He'd told them it was for him to sit on when he was visiting, but really it was to hide the thing.

Shivering, he looked at his wife's headstone that one of the boys had made for her.

"You remember them roses I got you one year? They're in bloom again. Never seen a prettier flower than them yellow ones. I'll bring you some the next time I come." He thought he heard her, his Sally, and waited for her to say something more. "Can you come out now, love? I miss you something terrible. I know you can talk to me, but I wanna hold you a little now and then."

I'm here, my Jacob. His heart fluttered in his chest when she spoke. *I have been thinking on why I'm not free like you are. It might be the earth is holding me for someone to find.*

"Who might that be? You tell me and I'll go and get them and show them where you are." Sally told him that she didn't think it would work like that. "You know who it is? Maybe one of the girls?"

I do. One of the women of our sons, perhaps. Or maybe none of them. But when I ask the earth to release me, they say that I will have to wait on a powerful love to come and free me. And before you ask, it's not you or the boys. He nodded, knowing that would have been too easy. *Are you reading still, Jacob? I would very much like for you to bring a book with you sometimes and read to me again. You have such a lovely voice.*

"I don't have much time right now, but I do read the backs of some of them boxes of sugary breakfast stuff that Essie eats. Do you know what is in that stuff?" She told him that she didn't even know what it was. "Flakes of corn, they say on the box. How the hell do you flake corn? And one of them has berries and nuts in it. Never seen a berry look like that before, except when it's been a dry summer and they're all dried up. But she loves it and I have a hard time not watching her enjoy it. You'd really like her, that one. Can make me smile the way she fusses on them boys of ours like they were her own. And she loves Asher too."

Jacob was thinking about the other things that his Essie enjoyed when his Sally spoke again. *She comes to see me, did you know that? Once a week, she comes out here and just sits. She never speaks to me as you do, and I'm not sure I can talk to her, but it's nice to have her so close and to see what her day has been. I really like her, Jacob, I truly do.*

"I do too, honey. I surely do. You should talk to her a little. Might do you both some good to do that. If it don't work, I think she'd still come to see you a bit." Sally said that she'd think on it. "I got me one of them reader things I was telling you about a few days ago. Well, Gideon got me one. Had to show me three times how to load things on it. Been playing some games on it too. One of them is a matching game, like the card games we played with the boys when they was younger."

If it's a reader, Jacob, you should be reading. Games are for children, not for grown men that have difficulty reading a corn flake box. He smiled at her tone, missing it even when she was reprimanding him for something. *You're laughing at me, aren't you? You know how much that makes my temper rise up.*

"I remember that temper of yours. Nah, I'm missing you. Something powerful too. I'll be glad when we can figure this here thing out, love. I want to hold you again." He looked toward the house and the bedroom he knew to be Jed's. "I sure hope Jed figures this out too. Gonna be in for a long haul if he don't. And if'n she dies, there will be nothing left for him, I'm thinking."

He will love her. Jedidiah is a good man. He'll not leave her to be hurt and unloved. Jacob hoped so. But he more hoped that she'd be all right. *And she will live as well. I know it."*

They were all good boys and better men than he'd ever dreamed they'd be. But this thing with Jed, it did worry him a mite, more than he wanted to admit even to his Sally. He leaned back on the ground and they talked for another hour. He missed her more and more every day, and decided that he'd be coming out more to talk to her. It made him feel like she was there with him instead of gone from him. Jacob loved his wife as much as he did their sons, and wanted her home too.

Having her die the way she'd done had never set well with him. One day she'd been putting up some beans for the long winter, and the next she'd been sick with a cold. And a week later, after it had settled up in her lungs, she'd been gone, his love, his heart gone with her. Jacob had sat with her for a week before he'd let them take her out and bury her. And he had a hard time, even now, knowing that she'd gone off without him. Sally and his children had been his entire life, and still were.

Chapter 3

Jed wasn't sure how to hold her in his arms and not touch her. It was stupid, of course, but he wasn't sure what she'd feel like if she woke up and a man who was only wearing a pair of jogging shorts was holding her. And he was hard as stone too. She was slippery, and they were having a hard time keeping her from falling to the stall floor.

"Hold her still. I don't want to get shampoo in her eyes." Jed glared at Zak. He'd told him the moment he came into the room that he was going to do the washing and Jed the holding. "Jed, have you never held a woman before? You act like you have no idea what to do with one, if you want my opinion."

"I don't, so keep it to yourself. And I have held onto one, but she's usually holding onto me, too, when I'm…when we're…just wash her damned hair." If Zak laughed at him once more, he was going to shove her into his arms and leave him. "Why do you think she's so small? I mean…we both can hold her with one hand."

"I don't think she's been eating all that well." Jed nodded. "And this wound has me worried too. The red streaks going up her leg can't be good."

"No. It's a sign of blood poisoning. We're going to have to try and get the poison out of her before it kills her." Jed wasn't really sure how to do that, but he did know that much. "Maybe I can, I don't know, suck it out of her."

Her breasts were plastered against his chest and the thought of sucking anything on her had him hurting again. She was thin and a little on the undernourished side, but she was most assuredly woman. And one he wanted to sample in the worst kind of way. He looked up at Zak when he didn't answer him.

He was looking at her like he was starved. And while Jed might have been jealous of someone else looking at her that way, all he could feel for Zak was need. Not for him, but for the two of them to share this woman. Good Christ, this was not helping him at all.

"I've never been with a woman before." Jed knew this, and they had talked about it before. Zak had never intruded on him making love to a woman, but he knew that he was there, watching them. "Do you think she'll be able to take us both? I mean, enjoy us?"

"Yes." Jed reached down to his cock and adjusted himself again. "Christ, we have to get this done. I'm ready to push her up against the wall and have her right now, I need her so much."

Washing her body nearly took him to the floor. And watching Zak scrubbing her, the sponge going up and down her lovely body, had him nearly sobbing. When Zak rubbed his cheek over her ass and moaned, Jed turned off the water and pulled her out with him. Zak told him he wasn't done just yet.

"Yes you are. You're killing me." He snarled at Zak when he asked him what he'd done. "You were touching her. Like sexually. I can't…what the fuck? I hurt like I've never been with a woman before, and here you are moaning like…like…well, like you want her too. And knowing that you want her as much as I do is not helping me one bit."

Jed took the towel from Zak and started to rub it over her. When she cried out, he realized how hard he was doing it and had to step back and take a breath. Never in all his life had a woman affected him like this one. And looking at Zak in the mirror, he could see that he was just as needy.

"We're going to hurt her if we go at her this way. I mean, when we make love to her, we're going to hurt her with our need." Zak asked him what they could do. "I'm not sure. But this isn't working. We have to figure something out."

"Jacob said that we should get in bed with her to warm her up." *Well, that wasn't the least bit helpful,* Jed thought. "I'm thinking that it might be a bad idea…what do you think? I mean, the thought of her being naked with us…I just think that's a bad idea."

"We have to get her healthy, and if that means we have to lie with her, then we do. We'll behave ourselves when we do." Zak asked him if he thought they could do that. "I have no idea, but we're going to do it."

Wrapping her gently in the towel made him feel better. Putting her in the center of the bed, he realized how small it was and reached for Asher. Telling him what he needed and why was embarrassing, especially when

Asher told him that closer was better. But as the bed stretched out for them, he tried his best to ignore the rest of his brother's advice.

When she wakes, I will tell you it could go one of two ways. The first, it will be wonderful. The second…not so much. She might tear you to ribbons before you convince her that you're her mate. And then it might be iffy. I'd say to bring her around with a climax.

Shut the fuck up. Asher laughed harder. *You know, right now I could gladly kill you and go to the chair with a smile on my face. I really hate you that much. More I think.*

And while you're sitting there with the electric going through your body, you'll have the biggest hard-on known to man. Jed growled. *How is Zak doing? The two of you ready to pounce on the first thing that touches you?*

Fuck off. He closed the connection between them and crawled into the bed, but had to get up to take off his wet pants and was thoroughly mortified by his erection. Getting under the covers helped some, but when he pulled her body to him, he nearly cried. Zak crawled in on the other side and wrapped his body around her too.

At first all he could think about was how much he wanted her. Then, as he began to relax, his body warming up with her, he thought of how much he wanted her to be better. Her body was warm, really, and when she began to shiver, he moved so that her body faced his and Zak curled around her backside. The three of them were as tight together as any one person could be to another, he figured.

"She'll be fine." Jed nodded at Zak. "I have a feeling that when she wakes up, she's going to tell us, without any problem, how much she appreciates us doing this for her. Don't you think so?"

"Are you assuming that she's going to be thrilled to find herself in bed with us?" Zak shook his head no and smiled. "Yeah, me either. If we're lucky she'll only hurt us and not unman us before we can…you know."

"You mean she'll try to harm us?" He sounded so shocked that Jed laughed. "I have no idea why, but I thought a woman would like to have two men in her bed."

"Not when they're strangers." Zak said he had a point, and he closed his eyes. Jed tried the same, making his body forget about the warm naked female that was nearly atop him. So he tried to think of the castle and what it was going to look like when they got it finished.

The stone had been cut over a period of several years, they'd found out. Jed had, with the help of Zak and Asher, figured out where they had mined the stone. The quarry that they'd referenced it to was now overgrown with trees and other foliage, and Zak had found a couple of places where he thought his parents might have used their own heat to break some of the larger pieces free. The dark stain on the walls of the rock looked old, of course, but it was there for them to see and that was great. They also speculated that perhaps they had even brought the stone to the growing building when there was no one around, carrying it in their massive claws to set it in place. It would have been easy for them as opposed to bringing it in by horse and wagon.

The forest the furniture had been built from was also overgrown. But they could see where someone had planted the newer trees, some of them centuries old, in straight lines, and that they had been, for a time, taken care of. No one had been in that forest for decades, they'd figured, and if they had been there, it wasn't to cut trees.

Deer and other animals were present in the area, a great deal of them. It made him think of a protected forest he'd been in a very long time ago, and he wondered what had ever happened to it.

Over the next few days they were going to have the entire place excavated of the fallen stone. The two walls that remained upright were helping in the fact that they could see how they were stacked. It had surprised them all that most of the back of the castle at one time had been built into the stone of the mountain behind it. He would bet anything that it had kept the keep at a constant temperature no matter the time of year. And they, too, were going to utilize that as a part of their home.

The castle was going to be bigger than the one that had sat there all those years ago. Not that there were more people to live and work in it, but they'd all decided that they'd have it bigger for their families to use. Asher and Essie were going to live in it, of course, but it was as yet undecided if any of the rest of them wanted to live there. Not that they'd not be welcome, but Gideon and Onimia had expressed a desire to live in their own home should they ever find a mate. Jed wondered what he and Zak would do now.

Jed yawned, only just realizing that he'd done it several times now. When he felt his body drifting to a very relaxed state, he knew that sleep wasn't far off. Jed was sort of nervous about falling asleep with her in his arms, knowing that she wasn't going to be happy when she woke up. He could only hope that either he or Zak, or both, would wake before her to make sure that they were well away from her when she finally did rise. In theory, it was a solid plan.

~~~
~~~

Lindsey felt warm. Too warm, actually, and she tried to move away from the heat even if only to cool off just a little. But then the front of her was warmed up by the rock that was there as well. She had no idea how the stones in the cave were this hot, but she might stay in here for the rest of her days just to bask in the warmth for a change. When she moved her hand to see if she could maybe shift over it, the rock moaned.

Opening one eye, she looked at the man lying on his back beside her. She was almost terrified to see what…or who…was behind her, but the man that she'd touched was looking at her now, and she opened her other eye. He had the most beautiful blue eyes, and his face looked like someone had sculpted it from the rock she'd been laying on. Or thought she'd been laying on.

"You're all right?" When she nodded to the man he smiled at her, and Lindsey felt her heart skip a beat or two. "We were worried about you. The wound on your leg was badly infected. We had to clean it up, and then Zak had to burn it a little to make it well again."

"Zak?" The body behind her moved, and she felt him rock into her bottom. Her body heated up, and she was sure it had nothing to do with the fever she'd had when she'd been in the cave. "I'm naked, aren't I? As are you, I'm betting."

"Yes. We're all naked. We had to keep you warm. You had a high fever." Nodding again, she felt sort of like a simpleton. "I'm Jed. Well, Jedidiah Benson, but only my mother called me that."

"And she is…?" He told her that she'd died some time ago. "I'm sorry. But you are…and I'm really trying my best not to freak out here, but you two decided all on your own that being naked with me in a bed would help me get better?"

"No. My dad thought it was a way to bring the fever down. And it worked for my sister-in-law, Essie, when she was sick." He shifted on the bed and his body was turned to hers now. His cock—she could feel it now—was right at her belly, and she wanted to move closer to it, and had to work very hard not to. "You're doing very well. I was afraid that you'd hurt us."

The man at her back moved his hand up from her waist to her breast. As soon as he cupped it in his hand, she felt her nipples pucker up and her breast tighten. When he tugged on her nipple, then rocked hard into her ass, Lindsey moaned. She had no idea what the man behind her looked like, but his hands were rough and big enough to cover her entire breast.

The bed shifted again, and she moaned when she was laid back. Her entire body felt hot when Jed moaned as the covers that were on them began their journey down her body. She didn't even try to stop the blanket, but watched the face of the man who was moving it. And when Jed took her other breast into his mouth, Lindsey curled her fingers in his hair to pull him back, but instead held him to her. The other man took her other breast and she nearly came apart.

Their hands were everywhere, touching her in places just long enough for her body to get worked up before moving to someplace else to touch her. When the other man moved up on his elbow and smiled at her, his hands running from hip to hip, she wanted to ask him if he was going to do more than touch her when he just stared at her. Lindsey wanted to beg him to go back to her breast, suckle on it enough to give her some relief, but he kissed her mouth. His tongue, slick and very quick, knew every part of her mouth before he lifted his head and moved to her breast again. Jed turned her to him, and he kissed her while the stranger moved down her body to her navel.

"Zak wants to taste you. Eat your pussy and see if he can make you come. Would you like that?" Lindsey had no breath to tell him that was a good idea because Zak sucked on her navel before moving down between her legs. "I will as well, when he's had his fill. I doubt we will ever be full of you, but he promised to share you. All right?"

"Yes. Please, I would like that very much." Jed kissed her, her legs were spread apart, and she felt Zak's breath on her heat. Her pussy soaking wet now, she tensed up for his touch. "I'm not sure that this is right. I've never…Christ, yes."

Her climax took her breath away, and when Zak sucked on her clit, she rode his mouth until she came again. His tongue fucked her; his fingers spread her wider as he ate her, devoured her like she was a fine piece of beef. Jed was at her breasts, sucking on one and then the other before nibbling on the tip until she wanted to sob. When she came again, this time screaming out Zak's name, she felt as if every part of her had been touched by them, inside and out. And it wasn't enough. Not nearly enough to satisfy her. She didn't think they were going to stop until she was dead, either. She wanted to touch them too, feel their cocks, even taste them if they'd let her. But when Jed lifted his head, she wanted to have him fuck her, his cock to fill her.

Jed said it was his turn, and he switched places with Zak. Lindsey had a thought. A small one that was there and gone before she could act on it. She was in bed with two gorgeous men, and they were making love to her. To her.

Jed ate her like he was in this for her pleasure only. His fingers entered her as Zak's had, but he twisted her up inside, touched off a spot in her that had her screaming out his name more than once. Lindsey came so many times that she felt as if she'd been wrung out and left to lay in the sopping mess. Reaching for something to hold onto when Jed began again, she felt a hard thick cock at her fingers and looked up at Zak when he sat on his knees beside her.

The need to taste Zak nearly had her forgetting the man between her legs. Fisting Zak, his cock slick with his precum, she begged him to come to her mouth. The bed moved as he positioned himself to have her beneath him, his knees on either side of her. She licked the tip of his cock even as she came twice more in Jed's mouth. When Zak was at her mouth, Jed lifted his head from her pussy, and she looked at him around Zak's hard body.

Cream dripped from his chin, his face covered in her juices. And when he leaned back on his heels, she could see that he was hard too, his cock longer than the impressive one near her mouth. Lindsey wanted them both. Licking Zak again, tasting him, she moaned as she watched Jed move around on the bed.

"Roll to your belly and when Zak is under you, like you are him, take him in your mouth and let him fuck that pretty mouth of yours. I'm going to take you here, slide my cock into you and fuck you." She did that as Zak moved to lay under her. Taking his cock into her mouth, she came quickly when Jed pulled her hips up off the bed and entered her from behind. Her pussy felt not just full from his cock, because he was huge, but something akin to being complete, the two cocks inside of her making her feel whole.

She was in heaven. A cock in her mouth that tasted of spicy heat and sex, and one in her pussy, pounding her gently but firmly stretching her was almost too much. Zak held her head, pushed her hair out of her way while he lifted his hips up and fucked her mouth. Her pussy was tight, filled over and over by Jed as he rubbed his hands up and down her back, fucking her. He was pulling at her breasts when he reached beneath her, touching her pussy just enough to make her moan around Zak's thick cock. When his fingers slid into her pussy, touching off another climax, Zak cried out his release, just as Jed sank his teeth into her shoulder and filled her too. Lindsey came with them, her mind nearly shutting down by the feel of the releases, hers included.

Exhaustion took her under, and she felt her body fall. Not far, because they had her, they kept telling her. Lindsey felt herself being lifted and cradled against a hard chest. She knew it was Jed, as his was hard and smooth, while Zak's was hairy and warmer. As she lay down again, her head on one arm, another around her waist, Lindsey wanted to tell them that was the best she'd ever had, but she couldn't seem to make her mouth work anymore. Falling into sleep, a soft and gentle drift, Lindsey felt the best she'd felt in all her life.

She woke some time later. The room was dark, and the small light coming from under the door somewhere made her think that it was the bathroom. Stretching out, she realized how incredibly sore she was and smiled. Then what she'd done hit her. She'd had sex with two men and didn't know a thing about them. The hand at her breast made her rock back into the hard body even as she told herself this was a mistake. She moved away from him when she realized what she was doing.

"Are you all right?" The voice…Zak. "Lindsey? What's the matter? A bad dream or something?"

"No. What am I doing here?" She looked for Jed and when the light went off, she heard the door open and there he stood. The moonlight coming in from the room he'd just left made his body a perfect outline of the incredible man. "I need to get up. And leave. I can't…what was I doing? Did you…was I drunk?"

"No. We can't drink. It affects our magic badly." Jed didn't come back to bed, so she moved away from Zak so that he wasn't touching her. His hands, his wonderfully talented hands, were making her want them both again. "I'm going to turn on the light, then we can talk, okay?"

She never got a chance to answer Jed as the light was turned on. She got her first look at the room and the two men that she'd spent hours making love with. It was their room, she realized; she was in their room in their bed. Swallowing twice, she tried to get her fear and her emotions under control.

"I don't do this. I mean, I have never done this before. And I don't do it when I don't know the men…man I sleep with either." Zak got up and went to the chair. She tried her best not to drool, but the man made her wet and he was not even near her right now. "I don't understand what happened here. I feel…well, the word overwhelmed does not even cover how I feel right now. I mean…Christ, I don't know what I mean."

"We had sex. A great deal of it too." Lindsey glared at Zak, and he smiled. "You're very beautiful when you're upset, and I'd like nothing more than to get back in bed with you and make love to you again. Woman, you are amazing. I'd like to fuck you now too, bury my cock inside of you and feel you tighten around me when I release. Can I?"

Ignoring the need to toss off the covers that were over her and tell them both to take her, she thought about what he'd said about her. No one had ever said that to her before, that she was amazing. And when she looked at Jed, he was nodding too. Embarrassed at how happy they'd made her, she tried to think what she'd been talking about. Sex. That was it. Sex.

"It wasn't our intention to make love to you until you got to know us better." Jed leaned back in the chair and stroked his cock. "I'm not saying that I didn't love every second of you, but we wanted to talk to you first. And like Zak, I'd like to make love to you again. Once was not nearly enough."

"Are you saying this is my fault?" He said no. "Then what are you saying? That you want me again? And you expect me to just let you? Both of you?"

"Oh yes. Yes, we both want you again. Badly, as a matter of fact." Jed stood up and walked to her—more of a glide, she supposed—and she felt her pussy swell with need for him. When he was close enough for her to touch, Lindsey sat on the edge of the bed, the covers forgotten, and reached up to wrap her hands around him as he rocked into her hand. "I really do want you again. Being inside of you, watching you come with my cock inside of you, is something that I want to see this time."

Zak came up behind her, wrapped his arms and legs around her, and cupped her breasts, tugging again on her nipples until she leaned back into him while fisting Jed's cock. When Zak lifted her and she came down on his cock, her pussy wet enough to take him despite his size and girth, Lindsey felt like this was what she'd been meant to do all her life. Please these two men.

"Suck me, Lindsey, while he fucks that pretty pussy of yours. Let him feel you when you come around him while I fuck your mouth."

Taking him to her mouth, she noticed the difference in their tastes right away. He rocked gently, taking his time she would bet. Zak held her breast in one hand and her pussy with the other. She rode him, feeling his breath on her neck as he kissed her, nibbled on her flesh as she grew closer and closer to the edge. His fingers played with her clit, tugging it as he was her nipples, her body on fire to come this way. This was amazing and made her feel sexy and loved. And when she came, screaming out her release around Jed's cock, he pulled her tighter to him and she tasted him.

His cum filled her mouth, slid down her throat even as she came again. Hands were everywhere again it seemed, not just on her breasts and pussy, but her back, her arms. She felt amazing, and came twice more before Jed pulled from her mouth and fisted his cock so that he came all over her, his hot cum feeling like a brand as it touched off another powerful climax.

When he dropped to his knees she didn't know what to think. He took her breast to his mouth and sucked hard, her pussy tightening again, and she heard Zak cry out. She wasn't sure if she was hurting him when he grabbed her hips, but right now she was building for something powerful, her body primed for one more climax that would kill her, she was sure. And when Jed told her to come, she felt his mouth at her throat, Zak on the other side. When she came, screaming now from the overwhelming pleasure of it, they bit her, each of them sinking their teeth deep into her throat.

Stars exploded behind her eyes. She felt torn apart then put back together with pieces of these men inside of her. Not just their cocks, even though that was more than enough, but more of them, parts of them that made her feel different. As she came again, this time not having the energy to even cry out, she knew that something was different. That somehow she'd changed…they'd changed her, and along with her, they had changed as well.

Lindsey didn't open her eyes when she was moved. Didn't protest when the water was pouring over her, only wondering briefly how she'd gotten in the shower. They washed her, their hands soothing her battered body even as they worshiped her. Everywhere they touched her, either with the sponge or their hands, it felt healing. Loving.

Being bathed then dried by the two of them, she listened to their words. They spoke of love, of her. Zak told her of a dragon and she remembered another one, not long ago. Jed told her of magic, his and now hers. They put her to bed, lying on either side of her, each of them holding her as she drifted once again into a heavy, deep sleep. There was no panic this time when she drifted off, no thoughts of what she was doing here, or what they were doing with her. Lindsey felt at peace, and that was all she needed.

Chapter 4

Zak moved the large boulder with his feet, dropping it several yards away in the pile of the ones they were going to use. It had been decided that they'd use what they could and replace the rest with stones from the same quarry that his parents had used. When he returned, he sat on the ground to await the next unearthed stone to take away.

Jed and he had talked long into the morning, using their connection so that no one would know what they said. Zak was overwhelmed by it all, if he was honest with himself, and he was with Jed about his feelings. Making love had been nothing like he'd thought it would be, and so much more than he'd dreamed.

She's beautiful. Zak had agreed. *But we have to go gently with her. She's not used to…well, this much. I mean, she's going to be sore, I think. Did you see the way she moved when we left her? Like she'd been made love to a little too much. Not that I didn't enjoy it as much as you did, but I don't want her aching like that again.*

I think she'll be all right. We both gave her some of our magic, and she'll heal quickly. Jed had asked him how he knew what they'd done, and he had no answer. He told him he just knew.

She tasted different this morning than she did last night. Zak had noticed that as well and had told him that. Both of them had eaten her, bringing her several times before he'd gotten to fuck her and Jed had his cock sucked. He wanted to have her between them, each of them inside of her, but there was time for that. *Could that be what you mean by knowing that she has some of our magic?*

I don't know, to be honest. He had taken a large boulder of stone away, and when he returned he thought of something else. *We have to talk to her, you know. I mean, whenever I'm near her, all I want to do is taste and touch her again, but we have to talk to her. Maybe we can make love to her to relax us and her, then talk. You think that'll work?*

No. She's very distracting. They both laughed, and Zak picked up the stone that Asher had asked him to move. But as he pulled it free, three of the larger stones near it shifted and he watched as the one in his claws slipped forward. It was crashing to the earth and toward his family almost faster than he could move. He moved to grab it again, but it was moving too fast.

Jed leapt at his brother and knocked him out of the way. If he had not then the stone would have come down on him and crushed him. Zak shifted quickly and called to Kiaran, who was taking one of the stones away too. As soon as Asher was pulled out of the deep pit and found to be all right but for a few scrapes and cuts, they all stood around staring at one another. It was the most terrifying few seconds of his life.

"I'm fine." They nodded, but no one was moving. "I really am. I shouldn't have been standing so close. It was my fault. I should have been—"

Essie seemed to come out of nowhere. She was in Asher's arms so quickly that Zak felt his dragon shift under his skin. It was as if he'd been startled as well. When she asked Asher several times if he was all right and got the same answer, she turned to look at him and Jed.

"Thank you." Jed asked her for what. "You saved him for me. You could…he might have…you saved him. I was picking mushrooms and I felt…well, like something was going to happen. I think the earth told me and I ran all the way here in time to see you…to watch him…you saved him."

After she hugged them, they stood back near where the stones had fallen through. They saw a pit there, which was the reason why the stones had fallen like they had and shifted when he'd pulled the one free. And it was deep, so deep that the sun didn't penetrate the darkness. Essie took off her shoes, and Zak thought for sure she was going to leap into the hole, but she raised her hands up to the sky and asked for light.

In small increments light began to fill the area. It was not just deep but wide as well. As the light filled it more and more, he could see that there were things hanging on the walls, tapestry's that looked to be in good shape for as old as they were. A chair at one point looked as if it were sitting on nothing until the light filled in the area behind it. A room. A bedroom, it looked like, with a large four poster bed sitting there with pillows still atop it.

More and more of the space below them took shape. Another room. A bed that had a stone in it. In several places the earth had spilled into the rooms, and the walls had cracked in another. The deeper the light went, the more the shape of the castle began to appear. Things from centuries ago, their parents' lives, showed themselves in a new light. Then they saw the stairs.

"Don't." They all looked at Lindsey when she spoke, startling them to take a step back from the opening. "I don't know what…please don't go down there."

Asher looked at Zak, then at Jed. There was something on his face, but he wasn't getting it. But Jed apparently did and smiled at them all.

"Lindsey, this is my family. You've met Casdon. These are my brothers, Asher, the oldest. Then in order of birth after me is Elam, Shane, Gideon, and Simeon. Their dragons are Kiaran with Asher, you know Zak." Her face brightened when she looked at him and Jed cleared his throat as he continued. "Keion with Shane, Onimia, and Akassa."

"Dragons." She looked at him, then at Jed before speaking again. "I'd like to talk to you two. Later. I mean, now would be good, but we have to talk later."

"All right." Zak wanted to go to her then, but she looked…well, upset. He glanced at Jed, who was telling her about what they were doing. Zak wasn't that good around women, and no matter what Jed had told him about his lack of good experiences with a female, he was doing well. Zak had no idea how to talk to them, and less about how to make them feel good about being around him. He did, however, move closer just to be near her.

"So you think something is down there?" She nodded at Essie but said nothing more to clarify things. "I don't feel anything. That's not to say that there isn't something down there. I just don't feel it right now. What is it that you can feel?"

"It's not really a feeling so much as…well, doom. I guess that's a feeling too. But I think something…someone wants you to go down there, and they don't feel very nice." Essie looked at Zak when Lindsey did. "I'm not sure what I'm doing here. Something told me to come here and stop you all from going down there, and now I'm…I don't know what to do with myself."

"You really do need to talk to them, I think, and soon." Lindsey nodded but continued to stare at Zak while Essie continued talking to her. "You will be staying here, so we'll have to go into town and get you—"

"No." Zak and everyone else moved as one to go to Lindsey, her fear projecting to all of them. Jed was on her right and him her left when she nearly screamed her denial. "I can't go into town. I mean, I could, but I don't want to. He'll find me again. I can't, I will not go back to his house. Not after tasting freedom."

Essie nodded but didn't push the issue. She'd be fine if she wanted to go, he'd talk to her about it, but for now Essie would calm her, Zak knew.

"All right, but I want you to know that he can't hurt you again. We won't let him. And if he tries, then he's as good as dead. We're family now, and we won't let anyone be hurt." Lindsey looked at him, then at Jed, and he knew she was questioning whether or not they'd do just that, and more than likely wondering why they'd protect her. But Essie spoke again and told her what he would have. "Yes, they'll keep you safe, as will any of us here. No one will hurt you again."

"Why not? I mean, why are you so sure of that?" Essie looked at Asher, then back at Lindsey as she continued. "You don't know me any better than they do, yet you sound like you know that no matter what, they'll lay down their lives for me. Why?"

"You know what they are, but what you don't know, and I'm sure that they'll tell you, is that Zak and Jed are your mates. The two of them are...well, like your husbands. They will do anything to keep you safe, the same as Asher and Kiaran do for me." Essie smiled at them as they stood there. "Lindsey, I promise you, you'll have nothing to worry about here."

"You sleep with them both too?" Lindsey took a step back from them after her outburst. No one said anything to her, but Zak could feel her embarrassment. "I'm not like this. I don't know what's going on here or why I'm like this with them. It's not that I don't enjoy them both, but I'm not that kind of person, one who just has sex with someone without knowing anything about them."

Her voice was low, but Essie heard her, as did he and Jed. Zak was pretty sure that the rest of them had as well, but they all turned and left the area, leaving only him and Jed and Essie, Asher and Kiaran standing with her.

"We're a family, love. We won't do anything to harm you or let anyone hurt you." Lindsey nodded, but Zak knew that she wasn't convinced by Asher's words. He wrapped his arms around her, and she leaned into his body. "Do you feel it? The connection with them both?"

"Yes. It's almost too much at times." Asher nodded and pulled Essie to him. Kiaran turned them both so that he could hold Essie from behind, but they still faced Lindsey. Jed joined them and held Lindsey in much the same way that his brother and Asher were Essie. "I've never felt this way before. Invincible, loved. I even feel like I have this strange power that makes me feel like I can take on the world and actually win."

"You do have powers. Not enough to take on the world so much, but anyone that comes to harm you. Jed has a power that he's more than likely passed on to you. Close your eyes." When she did, Asher continued in a soft but firm voice. "I want you to think of something you'd like to wear. A pair of boots, perhaps. A coat that you might like. How about a sweatshirt that has your college on it?"

Zak knew that she had the power when the boots appeared on her feet. He wondered what else she could do when his brother started to speak in the same low but firm tones.

"Think of lifting from the ground now. Your feet are no longer touching it and you can feel the wind in your hair. Do you feel it, Lindsey?" She said that she did and Zak held her tighter as the three of them started to rise up from the earth. "You have no wings, but you have the ability to rise up and float just above the trees. You'll be able to see for miles. Keep yourself safe by taking to the trees should you feel threatened and no one else is around. Do you feel better? Lighter?"

He knew the exact moment when she opened her eyes. Her body was stiff, and he knew they were going to fall to the earth hard. Shifting while holding onto her and Jed, he held them in his claws as he took to the skies. Soaring upward, he could hear her laughter as well as Jed's as they landed in his favorite place of all the areas around them.

~~~

Jed watched her closely. It was too much for her, he knew that, and he was pretty sure that Zak did as well. As she looked around, he sat down on the ground near Zak and reached out to rub the dragon behind the ears. He purred as he always did.
~~~

"My name is Lindsey Decker. I'm…I'm trying my best not to run screaming from all this that's going on here. But I thought after all the time we've spent in bed together you should know that." Jed didn't say anything but continued to watch her. She wanted to talk, and he was going to let her. "I was…when your brother found me, I was looking for a new job when this ad came out in the paper about a housekeeper. I needed something, as I'd been out of work for a few days and I'm not one to sit idle well. So I applied for it and had an interview set up."

"What did you do before?" She didn't look at them, and he was okay with that, for now. "And if you don't mind me asking, why were you unemployed?"

"I'd been a receptionist for a doctor's office before. I knew crap about medicine, but I was good at answering the phone and filing. I didn't go to college like your brother said, but I was going to night school to try and better myself. It was hard sometimes, balancing buying books or food. And the places I've lived have been less than…nothing like what you guys have. Anyway, the office shut down when the doctor's wife caught him with one of his nurses. I guess she wasn't the first woman he'd been with and she took him to the cleaners. But before that I just worked. Whatever I could find to keep me in money, a place to live, and food to eat. Not necessarily in that order, either." Her fingers danced along a tree branch. Innocent, he supposed, but all he could think about was how she'd touched him…her fingers touching him the same soft way. Clearing his throat, he asked her about the job with Cox.

"The paper said it was a simple housekeeping job. I knew how to clean up after myself and thought that it would be all right until something better came along. And if it didn't, then it would pay the bills for a time." Jed asked her what the interview consisted of. "General questions. Now that I think on it, he was very concerned about making sure I had no family. Not just none in the area, but none at all."

"He wanted to make sure no husband or family came looking for you would be my guess." She nodded, still looking off in the distance. "What made you take the job? I mean, to work for a single man would be scary in and of itself, I'd think."

"He had a woman there when I was there to interview. She was nice enough. Sort of on the quiet side, but smiled a lot. I know that sounds really stupid of me, taking a job because someone smiled a lot. But I did. And having a woman there, for whatever reason, made me feel sort of safe, I guess." Her movements were slower; she was thinking, and he knew that. "I showed up the first day and he said that he'd forgotten to go to the store to get cleaning things. Seemed strange, but I told him I'd come back. The house really wasn't that bad, but it did smell kind of old. So I agreed to come back the next day. He told me that he'd be ready by then. He was ready for me, all right. Within minutes of being there, I knew I'd made a terrible mistake and was never going back."

Jed knew that the man had hurt her. He was pretty sure that in addition to chaining her up, he'd beaten her too. But he waited for her to tell him, so that when he found this fucker, Jed could make him pay for everything he'd done to her. Even things that he might have thought of doing to her. Zak laid his head near his leg, and he could see the tension in his body too, as if he knew what he'd been thinking.

"I cleaned the first bathroom anyway. I didn't want to set him off. I have no idea why I thought he had a temper, but I was careful not to be in the same room with him. I suppose I should have just left, but I didn't want a bad reference. The woman wasn't around, but I could see her things. A hairbrush in the bathroom, hair things in the bedroom, as well as clothing. So I didn't get too worried, not even when he asked me to *whip* him up a sandwich." She moved to sit down now, her back to the tree so that she was facing them. But she didn't look at them as she told her tale. "The sandwich wasn't right, he told me. I'm not sure what about it was wrong, but he swept the plate and the glass of tea he'd poured himself off the table. Then he stood up quickly and backhanded me. While I was down—I don't think that I lost consciousness—but before I knew it, he had a chain around my throat and a whip in his hand. Then he pulled my shoes off for some reason."

"He didn't want you to be able to run. He might have figured that without them, you'd not think of trying to escape." She nodded. "The woman, was she still there later? After she showed up, did she try to help you?"

"She's dead." Jed looked at Zak as the chill ran down his spine. He'd done this before was all he could think about. "I didn't see her or her body, but he told me that he'd gotten tired of her fucking up...his words, not mine. And that it was time for fresh blood. I had a feeling that he meant that—fresh blood—but I didn't know for sure. He...he would whip me daily with this whip-like thing he had. I think that it's called a cat o' nine tails. There were burrs at the end of each piece of leather that would bite into my skin when he used it. He often told me I took it better than any of the others."

"Others?" She didn't answer him, and that frightened him more than he could say. Before he could think of how to ask her again, she began speaking.

"I had to find something once. He'd told me it was in the attic and he had his hand on the chain when I went up there. I could see the boxes then." He wanted to ask her about them, what had frightened her so much about them, but she changed the subject. "I never got to eat much. Not that there wasn't food, but he wouldn't let me have any of it. Sometimes he'd give me a bone from his meal that I tried hard not to eat, but after a while, starvation won out."

"How long were you with him?" Zak was sitting with him now, as a person and not his dragon. Jed worried about him too. Not that he'd hurt any of them, but he could see the murderous look in his eye when he asked about the man.

"Just over a year. The other day when Casdon found me, it wasn't the first time I'd gotten away. But this is the longest I've been gone." She looked at them both now. "The day that I got away, he'd tried to have sex with me. Well, not intercourse, but he wanted me to have oral sex with him. He said that he'd missed that I was ripe. That word, ripe…it scared me more than the thought of having sex with him did. I punched him in the balls, and when he fell back, he hit his head on the table. I took the key that he had around his neck and gathered what few things I could and left. I've been running since."

"You didn't want to go to town. Why not?" Jed watched her face as he waited on an answer. The emotions were rolling over her fast, and few of them were anything close to being happy. "You didn't just not want to go, but you seemed to be terrified to go."

"He's a cop. Or he said he was. The few times that he had one or more of his buddies out to the house, I could see their cruisers and hear them talking, but couldn't make out what they were saying." Zak asked her where she'd been when this was happening. "The basement. He had a cell down there, kind of an old fashioned jail cell just like you'd see on television, and he told me, over and over, should I yell or make myself known to them, he'd give me to them just before he shot me in the head like he'd done to Donna."

"Do you know where he lives? I mean, could you find it again from this point?" She stood up, and he did as well. "We can take you over the area if that helps. Well, Zak can. I can help you with your appearance, but not flying."

"Appearance?" Jed nodded and put out his hand. As he changed it from large to small, dark then light, nails long then short, she watched him. When she put her hand out, he watched her struggle with trying to do it too. "You did the clothing thing, didn't you?"

"No. You did it. Just don't try too hard. Just think of making yourself look like someone. It has to be a person that you know. You don't want to try to be something that you might mess up if challenged." She closed her eyes, and he looked at Zak. The smile on his face was priceless when she made herself look like Jed. "That's not very nice. What if I became you?"

He didn't morph into her but into Asher. Zak was laughing now, and he could tell that Lindsey was feeling better as well. She turned in the direction of the castle, as it was easy to make it out from here, and then looked to the south. He could see a tiny curl of smoke coming up and wondered if it was him.

"I'll go and have a look. I remember what he looked like, and Casdon said he'd meet me at the ruins. We're going to go and see if he's on our property. I know that it's really all ours, but to see if he's going beyond the boundaries that were set out for him." Zak changed to his dragon then back again, pulled Lindsey to his body, and kissed her. When she was let go, she leaned against Jed as Zak took off. Jed held her until he was out of site.

"He's not going to get hurt, is he?" He told her he wouldn't do anything too stupid. Casdon would keep him out of trouble. "I'm falling in love with you two. I know that sounds stupid after only a few hours together, and most of that fucking, but I have."

"We made love. We were not just fucking. Though there are times when I'd like nothing more than to just fuck you, like right now." She turned in his arms, and he leaned in and kissed her. "And I've fallen in love with you too, Lindsey. I want you. Now, here in the woods. I don't think there will ever be a time when I don't want you. Even if it's only to hold you."

She wrapped her arms around his neck, and he lifted her. Thinking about her being bare to him, he felt the moment that her clothing disappeared. Her pussy, wet and hot, was snug against his belly, and his cock felt wet in the breeze. Lindsey was theirs, now and forever.

He took her to the tree he'd been leaning against earlier and lifted her enough to suckle at her breasts. Her fingers pulling at his hair to keep him there had him wanting her more, needing more of her. Jed wanted to drink from her again. He wanted to fuck her and eat her too, but knew that as hard as he was, as desperate as he felt, he'd come the moment she touched him.

As soon as he pulled her down over his cock, impaling her over him, Jed fucked her hard. The tree she was against shook with the power of his need, and he couldn't seem to slow, much less stop. Feeling her dig her nails into his flesh had his balls tight to his body. When she leaned into his neck, he thought that he'd die from pleasure when she licked his pounding pulse. And when she bit him, Jed felt his cock explode inside of her as he emptied deep. Even as she sucked at the wound, taking a part of him inside of her mouth, his cock filled again. He fucked her this time, pounded deep until he felt his climax take him over the edge and toss him away.

Jed held her. He knew that she'd come. Her body had tightened around him several times, but he felt bad for hurting her. He knew that she was sore and hadn't wanted to hurt her more, but Christ, the woman was amazing. Looking down at her, seeing her face relaxed after what they'd done, he smiled.

"We will never be able to be in public." He asked her why. "Because when either of you touch me, I want to slam you against the nearest hard surface and have you take me. Will Zak be like this? Will he…will he be upset that we didn't wait on him?"

"No. I don't think so. And if you and he are together and a hard surface is close, you should take him too. We both love you very much. You belong to us both, and us to you." She nodded and looked away. He brought her face back to his and looked deep in her eyes. "We both love you, Lindsey. And we're not in competition for you. If you want us both or not, we're going to be happy to have you in our lives. Forever."

"What happens when you get tired of me?" He kissed her nose. "You might. I mean, look at you. Do you have any idea how gorgeous the two of you are? Hell, all of you are like a wet dream to a woman. And I'm simply…well, just me. Plain old Lindsey Decker. Unemployed and homeless."

"I don't care if you ever want to go to work, but if you do, then that's all right with me too. As far as homeless, you're not. And plain? You are far from plain, love. Christ, you're the most beautiful creature I've ever seen. And where we live, that's where you live too. No matter what. I have several homes that I'd love to show you, and we'll get to all of them over the next few decades or so. I'm nearly three thousand years old, Lindsey. So is Zak. We've been waiting for you our entire lives." Her face was comical, and he nearly laughed when he realized what he'd said to her. "You didn't know that we were…how old we were."

"No. Should I have?" He let her go when she moved to be freed. He dressed himself when she did and watched her pace back and forth. Even after having her twice, he wanted her again and felt the touch of Zak just before speaking to her again.

He's on our land, just as we thought. A tenant that Elbert was telling us about. His family has been here a very long time I think, too. He asked him if the man was home and could he see anyone there. *There's a cruiser in the yard just like she said, but I don't think it's running. It looks old and dusty. Like it's been parked there for a long time.*

You think it's something he might use to scare women into behaving? He said that he thought so, and so did Casdon. *I'm going to tell Asher when we get back to the house. You should come here and talk to Lindsey. I think she's upset with me. I told her how old we were, and I'm not sure she believes me.*

What would I say to her? Zak sounded panicky, and Jed had to smile. *I don't know what to say to women, you know that. Just bring her home and I'll sit while you talk to her.*

You can't just have sex with her without conversation. He said that he could try. *No, you can't. Besides, we made love up here and now she's worried that you might be mad at us. She seems to think you're not going to be happy that I made love to her without you.*

Why would I be mad at the two of you? Hell, if I was there, I'd take her too. Jed told him good idea. *No. I'm not going to come there and talk to her. I don't know what to say to her. Don't do this to me, Jed. I'm not any good at this.*

Well, I'm leaving her here with the understanding that you're coming for her. If you leave her up here, she's going to be pissed off. Zak told him not to do it. *It's done.*

Zak was still screaming at him when he spoke to Lindsey. He told her that he was going to go back to the house, and that Zak wanted her to wait there for him. She seemed to be all right with that and he told her not to leave. He also told her about the house and the cruiser in Cox's yard.

"I won't leave. I love it up here. I can see the world from here." He kissed her again, holding her a few seconds longer before he moved down the hill. He was about halfway down when he saw Zak overhead, his great dragon blotting out the sky for several seconds. Waiting until he was sure that he was with Lindsey, Jed went home thinking about the man at the house. He was going to pay for his treatment of other women, and especially his woman.

Chapter 5

Brandon had put another ad in the paper three days ago. He watched for it to come out and when it didn't, he called down to the newspaper to find out what the hell was going on. They had him on hold for five minutes before someone came back on the line.

"Mr. Cox? There's a problem with your ad. I'm sorry. We have been trying to call you but you didn't answer." He tried to think if anyone had called, and remembered the half dozen private numbers that had come up on his caller ID. There were messages too, but he couldn't retrieve them, not without the password. "Are you there?"

"Yeah, I'm here. I have been having phone problems." He could have told her that the phone belonged to one of the many dead women in the yard and hidden in the caves, but he didn't think she'd like that all that much. "Your number, it comes up private. I tend not to answer those calls. Might be someone I don't want to talk to."

"Oh, I can understand that. I have a few of those come up too. But to get back to your ad, there is no mention of your name and who to ask for. And so you know, if a number comes up that you don't know, you might want to answer it. It might be someone looking for the position." Her little laughter grated on his nerves. He hated twitter laughs. That's what he called it when it sounded forced, like they'd twittered, not laughed. But he laughed with her, just to be polite. "What would you like for me to put down for that?"

It took him several seconds to remember what she'd asked him about. "Brandon, just my first name. I don't want any crackpots calling me for the job. So just my first name."

She told him it would be in the paper in two days. She even told him that it would run an extra few days at no charge since they'd not been able to put it in at the time they'd agreed upon. Now all he had to do was sit and wait.

Brandon was still pissed about Lindsey. She'd been working out so well, and then she had to up and run off. He supposed that it was sort of his fault that she'd wanted to go. One of his rules was no sex until they were properly broke in. And she'd not been there long enough for that as yet.

But by golly, she'd been pretty standing in the bowl with her bare body just slick with water—his water that he'd told her not to use. But she'd been fine, and that meant a lot more then. He'd wanted to take her against the table, just fuck her until he emptied himself in her, but she'd opened that pretty mouth, and all he could think about was fucking it instead. Yes sir, fucking her mouth would have gotten him off really quick.

He'd seen the look on her face when she'd seen his cock. He knew he was small. But he wasn't without some talent. Brandon could make his cock do things in a woman that would make her squeal with delight. At least that's what he'd been told. And why would they lie to him?

Laughing, he went out on the porch again to take in the night air. Brandon just loved it out here in the woods. He'd grown up here, born in the back bedroom, so he knew this place better than most. Even his parents before him had been born around here. His dad had told him that a lot over the years. Everyone was family, he'd said.

His parents and their parents before them had lived here forever, it seemed to him. Not that he'd cared all that much for his mom. She'd been a nasty sort of woman and blamed him for every little thing that had gone wrong. But Brandon had gotten the house when his dad had passed, and he'd put his mom in one of those nursing homes that the state ran.

Brandon was still getting her check, of course. He couldn't do much without her pension check, which he never understood, as neither of his parents had ever worked so far as he knew, but it was his now so he didn't worry about it. He'd put her in the home under a false name so that the state wouldn't come after it. It wasn't like she knew who she was anyway. And she had no reason to use the check he'd been cashing. It was his money, as he'd put up with her for years.

"Stupid woman." He sat on one of the large chairs that had been in the living room until he'd been able to snag a newer one. This one still had a lot of life in it, and he saw no reason to burn it just yet. Besides, he loved sitting out here on the cusp of the evening just relaxing to the sound of the crickets and cicada in the summer months.

Lindsey was out there somewhere, and he'd yet to find her no matter how much and hard he worked at it.

That bothered him to no end. If she went to the police, they'd come here again and question him. Twice they'd been here when she was, and like a good girl, she'd not said a word. But he had warned her, and that had seemed to work. However, if she found out that he not only didn't work for the police and was an ex-con to boot, she'd have his ass in trouble so quick he'd not be able to hide out this time.

Over the years since his daddy had died, Brandon had been in trouble. Even before then, he supposed, but he'd been a minor then, and after Daddy had died, he'd gotten worse. But he missed him, and missing him was what got him into trouble. Nobody seemed to understand that.

But about fifteen years ago, he'd done the wrong thing to the wrong girl, they'd told him. Never touch somebody that don't want it. He'd been having that drilled into his head since then. No means no. Then after five years in the big jail place, he'd been set free and had come back here to live.

But he still believed to this day that had she not made fun of his cock, he might not have hit her so hard…or that many times. She'd had no reason to laugh. And hurting her had brought the law down on his head so quickly that he was sure they were just waiting for him to mess up.

But Lindsey didn't laugh at him. He knew that she'd been shocked, but she didn't laugh. Which was a good thing. Donna hadn't either, but he could not have two women fighting over him, so he'd had to get rid of one of them. And since Donna was starting to get a little old for him—she had to be pushing thirty by the time he'd killed her—he'd decided to keep Lindsey around. That had been a mistake, he realized now. Lindsey had run off when he'd told her never to do that. And she wasn't as good at making him lunch as Donna had been either. Things with her, they just weren't the same as with the other women.

Brandon watched as the deer came out to eat. The salt was out there for them to nibble on, and come winter, when he was hurting for some meat, he'd go out and shoot one of them for a nice meal or two. He didn't have him an icebox like he used to, having had the one go to shit on him about four years ago. But the river worked out nicely for that come the cold, or in summer because of the mountain run off. He was, and he knew it, too lazy to have too much around to eat on, because he'd have to travel to the river bed to get it, and then haul it back. Sometimes he'd just eat whatever he could find, and that wasn't always all that good either.

Going into the house, he picked up his gun and the flashlight. He set off as he tucked the whip in the back of his pants as a backup. It was time to go hunting for her again. He figured that at night, when it was too dark for her to run, she'd settle down somewhere and he'd come up on her.

She'd be starved about now too, he figured. The little bit she'd taken wouldn't have lasted her this long. He wasn't happy that she'd found her bow and arrow set. She was good at it too…that girl could bury one of the arrows in a tree so as he'd not be able to take it out. It wasn't like it wasn't hers and all, but she'd snooped in his house and that was what had made him mad at her. It was his business, not hers.

The moon was behind some clouds when he started out. It took him a bit to find his way, and when he'd found himself near one of the caves, he started to poke his head in but heard the sound again. There was something down in there, and even during the day he'd not go in. If she was in there, good riddance to her. He wasn't going to go deep in the belly of the mountain again for no reason.

He knew that there were bodies down there. His granddaddy used to tell him of the dragons that used to darken the sky when his too many great-grandparents to remember had been living here. The house, he'd told Brandon, still belonged to the family and they had to pay a tax yearly, but Brandon had never been notified of a tax and had never paid up. Even if he had been, he wasn't so sure that he owed anybody anything. The place was his and his family's, as he'd been told his entire life.

Then about six months ago, some guy had come to the house telling him about his back payments or some such. But Brandon had told him he'd have to talk to his momma. She was the one with the money. The man had been back twice more in that time, but Brandon had hid from him in the cellar of the house. He was real careful of people coming around to collect on one thing or another.

It was nearing the sun coming up when he headed back to the house. He'd not found her again, and that sort of made him a little pissy. He did notice that someone was living in the big house on the back land, but he didn't venture near it. That was another place he'd been warned about as a kid. The house was said to be haunted. And that was something he was more than a little afraid of, hauntings.

By the time he got back to his house, it was full daylight. Disappointed that nobody was there to fill his belly, Brandon ate himself some fried eggs, but he ended up tossing two of them out because he'd broken the yolks. He liked his dippy eggs and wouldn't eat eggs any other way. Lindsey had done them up perfect for him every time, and she'd even made him hash browns when he'd been able to steal himself a potato or two. Thinking of her again made his temper rise up, but he was too tired to do much about it right now. But when he found her, he was going to lay out some new rules, and she was going to follow them or, by golly, she'd pay the price again.

Crawling into bed after tossing the plates in the sink, he thought of all the work that he'd have to do before the new housekeeper came to work. He wanted her to see how he wanted things, and that way they'd start off on the right footing. Brandon wished like hell that one of the others were there now. It looked better to have a housekeeper when there was a woman around looking for a job. That way they weren't too scared off by the time he had them where he wanted them. But there was no hope for it now if he didn't find Lindsey in time. Damn it all to hell and back, she was proving to be cagey.

Closing his eyes, he tried to sleep. The room was cold again, and he wasn't going to go out and get firewood to warm up. Pulling the blanket around him, he thought about having one of the housekeepers make him some quilts like his grandmother had, but he wasn't sure that he had the fixings for that. There were boxes of clothing up in the attic, as well as purses and stuff that he'd saved from all the other housekeepers, but he'd only get into them if he had to. The money was all gone, of course, and the credit cards were all in a box under the porch leg so nobody could steal them from him. His mother's things, he knew, were still in the cupboard. They'd do nicely.

Thinking about his plan must have worn him out because the next thing he knew, it was night again and he was feeling pretty good about things. Yes, sir, things were looking good for Brandon Cox.

~~~
~~~

"But you don't know what you felt when you said not to go down the stairs." Asher watched Lindsey's face. He knew that she wasn't lying, not that, but he could see that she was struggling with something. And while he knew that it had taken the three of them—he, Essie, and Kiaran—some getting used to, being together as a couple...trio...he didn't think that Lindsey, Zak, or Jed were having such problems. They looked...settled, for lack of a better term.

"No. It was like...you know that feeling you have when you think you've done something before? Or that you've heard it before?" Asher told her *déjà vu*. "Yeah, that's it. I had a feeling that I'd been down there before, and things were too creepy for me to get to remember. Understand?"

"Yes. As a matter of fact I do." She nodded but still looked upset. He decided that they'd talked long enough about the ruins. "Can you tell me a little about Cox? I mean, what he did to you? Some of the things he might have said? And by the way, he's not a cop. He has that car there because one of his relatives had gotten it in an auction."

"Jed told me the other day when we were at the hill. But the cops, they were at the house when he had me chained up in the basement. I couldn't hear them, of course, but I did see them. A cruiser was there as well as...I want to say four of the policemen, but I could only see one car besides the one that was in his yard." She got up to start pacing, and Asher watched her.

Jed and Zak were in town checking on some shipments that they were expecting, as well as picking her up some clothing. They had taken her sizes from her other clothing and were going to surprise her with them. Essie thought it was a good idea, but told them not to get too many personal things. They might overwhelm her again.

Neither of them wanted to leave her, but she refused to go with them, even after she was shown how she could change her appearance. Fear could make her magic a little unstable, and as she wasn't used to it yet, Jed didn't push her very hard. His grandda and his dad walked in the room just as she stopped moving and stood by the window. Neither of them said anything when Asher shook his head at them.

"When I was first there, the very first day, he was really nice in the morning when I started working. I had already decided that I wasn't going back after that. I mean, he's sort of crude in a backwoods sort of way, but he creeped me out. The woman that had been there before was gone, but he said that she'd gone herb hunting. Anyway, while I was washing up the dishes, he was puttering around the kitchen and he asked me to make him some lunch." His dad looked at Asher again before Lindsey continued. He knew as well as Asher did that she'd been hit, or worse. "He was pissed that the sandwich I made had tasted off. I'm not really sure what he thought I was going to do when he hit me, but I couldn't seem to get my body working well to get out of the house. He was big, even if he was stupid. The sandwich was just that, a sandwich, and when he knocked the plate and the glass to the floor, I knew that I was pretty much fucked about getting a good reference from him. I might have hit my head on something then. I'm not really sure. But I was hurting all over where he'd backhanded me. I didn't remember anything after that for a while when he hit me again."

"He chained you up then, to the floor?" She nodded but didn't go into any more detail. "Lindsey, I'm not asking you this to upset you, but the more information we have, the easier it will be for the police, the real ones, to take him in."

"I know that. But I'm still having a hard time trying to figure out why you'd care that much about me." She glanced at him, then away before continuing. "I was really stupid for taking the job in the first place. But I was hungry and needed some money for a hotel or something to sleep in. The nights were beginning to get cold back then."

"Did he ever tell you what happened to the other woman?" Asher waited for her to look at Grandda when he spoke, but she continued to stare out the window. He knew that she could see the garden, and Essie working in it with one of his brothers.

"No. Not right away, but he did tell me that she'd worn out her welcome. I wasn't sure what he meant. Maybe he'd sent her home, but when I asked, he told me that he'd had to kill her. Just like that, he'd had to kill her. He'd shot her in the head and told me he'd do the same to me should I run." Lindsey laughed a little. It sounded bitter and cold to him. "Every day, and I mean every day, I'd wait for some other woman to show up and him put a bullet in my head or whatever he did to the other women."

"You said women." Lindsey looked at his dad when he spoke. "You said other women, not woman. Do you know for sure there were other women?"

"Yes." This time before she continued, she came and sat back down on the chair she'd been in before. Her face was paler than it had been, and Asher was suddenly fearful of her answer. "In the attic he has these boxes. All of them are labeled with names as well as dates. Some of them have been up there for a little over ten years. I got a chance to look in them once. I don't remember why I'd been sent up there without the chain on me that time, but I was curious about so many of them. So I opened a few of them. There is clothing in the boxes. Some of them have blood on them, others just dirt. Purses, too, with shoes and hats."

"What else?" She looked at Asher, and he could tell she was terrified. "We won't let anything happen to you, Lindsey. Not ever."

"My box was marked too. Just my first name, like the others were. And while it was empty of my clothing because I was still wearing it, my things were in it. My apartment keys to the place I no longer stayed at, a purse that I'd come with, as well as the application that I'd filled out. He was keeping it to…when he killed me, he was going to put the ending date of my welcome and then put my clothing in it." Elbert asked her how many boxes were up there. "Eleven counting mine."

No one said a word. But if the others were thinking as hard as Asher was, then there wasn't any room for words at the moment. Ten women in ten years. And Lindsey had been with him just over a year. Her time, as he was pretty sure she'd already figured out, was running out. Her "welcome," as she'd called it, was about over too.

When she left them to go out into the yard with Essie, Asher warned his mate to go lightly and not to ask her too much. When she asked him what was going on, he told her what he had surmised and she said she'd take care of her. His dad got up to go to the window and told him that the girls were headed to the ruins, it looked like.

"You think that…he's killed ten other women and nothing has been done about it?" Asher nodded at his grandda. "Do you suppose the police being out there that day, they might have a clue what he's about?"

"I have someone looking into whether or not he's served time. I think, being that they were out checking on him, that he might have." Asher leaned back in the chair and regarded the two men in front of him that meant the world to him. "If he finds her out and about, he'll take her again and simply kill her. And whoever is with her when he does find her. Casdon said that he's still looking for her but not in town. I don't know why, but…well, he's not very smart, but I wonder why no one has asked after these women."

"Maybe he looks for girls that have nobody else in their lives." Asher had thought of it and was glad that his dad had as well. "I mean, he has them fill out an app, she said. Maybe he's looking for the perfect girl to come in, and then when he's had enough of them, he doesn't have to worry about their family showing up."

"You think that…Christ, this is horrible to think of, but do you suppose that the last woman is buried on the property?" Grandda said that was a safe bet. "The property is part of this estate. The lawyers are trying to get him to pay his due. Did you know that it's only one dollar an acre? And that it has to be paid on the fifteenth of October of every year? How the hell has he never been asked to pay that before now? It's so very little when you think of it."

"Yeah, now that you mention that, I remember that coming in. Back when you guys were little, the money went in a pot that would buy something that was needed should one of the others need a new roof or whatever."

His dad grinned. "We never needed the money…the king, he provided for us very well and we never hurt for anything. But the money did help out a few of the people living around here back then. How many tenants do we have here now?"

"Seven counting Cox. Most of them are just using the land to hunt or camp on in the fall and nothing else. I've had the attorneys find out if they want to sell out. We'd do well not to have other people around now that we've decided to make this our home. Not much in the way of acreage, mind you…the biggest one is ten acres. Cox has five, so he should have been paying five bucks a year and hasn't since…well, I think they said about ten years now." Asher picked up the paper in front of him he'd been making notes on and read it. "Yes, here it is, five acres. And the last of the tenants is a man whose family has lived here for as many generations as we have, but he's the last of them. Once he passes on, the property and the house will revert back to the estate."

Asher had never taken any notice of the legalities of the property before. He knew that there were people living on the land. Although he didn't know the exact amount, he knew they had to pay too. His attorney had mentioned once, a while ago, that one was behind, but if he mentioned it again, Asher couldn't remember the outcome of it. Now he was taking a big interest in it, if for no other reason than to take care of things for Lindsey.

"Dad, I just don't know what to do. We can call in the cops, but what if these women just left on their own and he decides to take revenge out on Lindsey or us? We would be a laughingstock. Not that I'm worried about us, but he could make it hard on her." His dad asked him why it would be any harder on her. "Lindsey has had some legal problems of her own. And some of them could get her into some serious problems."

"What kind of problems could that nice girl have? I'm telling you right now, if someone is telling lies on her, I'm not going to be happy. I swear to you, she's one of the nicest people I know." Asher knew that Lindsey liked his dad and grandda as well. "She ain't said nothing to Jed, either, if it's real bad. Not that I know of, anyhow."

"She's been in jail twice that I have found. Once for shoplifting, but that I can understand. It was food and she told the police that she was starved. And recently she was arrested for her part in a scam for money." Asher handed his dad the paperwork he'd been given just yesterday. "She has claimed from the start that she had nothing to do with it, and that the man that she was supposed to have gotten in trouble with wasn't her boyfriend like he'd told the police. But she did spend thirty days in jail. I can't find any more about it or the man she was with."

"You're thinking that she might have jumped bail or something." Asher nodded at his grandda, impressed that he'd know that. It wasn't that his grandda was stupid or backward, but he didn't get out very much, nor did he watch any television that he knew of. "I believe that our best course of action on that is to wait and see if she mentions it. It might be less than you are thinking, and if it is more, then we will protect her as best we can. She is family now."

As his grandda left the room, his dad stood up and moved to the window with the file still untouched in his hand. Asher watched his father. He was, as far as Asher was concerned, the greatest man he knew. And he had a great deal of respect for whatever he said. Today was going to be no different in helping him deal with what was going on with Lindsey.

"I believe you are right in not calling in the police. That doesn't mean that we don't go looking for things on our own, but we're going to do it using magic and not the police for now." Asher told him he liked that idea. "And we will talk to Lindsey, as a family. Tell her what has come our way and we will believe whatever it is she has to say on this. As Elbert has said, she's our family now."

"All right, I can do that. Essie and I can talk to the earth when she gets back. Together our magic is a good deal stronger and we can reach further out." His dad nodded and came back to hand him the file. "Dad? What about the rest?"

"Like I said, we talk to her. It's what a family does. We don't accuse, nor do we assume. That will hurt us and her more than anything else we can do. For all we know, she might have told Jed and Zak already, and if not, it's her plan to do so. We'll do this her way."

After he left, Asher reached out to Essie. She told him they were fine, but she didn't want to come in just now. *I think she just needs to know that we're here for her, and even though she's not talking, we're communicating.*

He didn't understand her but told her that he loved her very much. After she closed the connection, Asher set to work. His businesses were getting to be a little too much right now, and as much as he wanted to blow them off and go find his wife, he knew that just putting off the work would only make more of it for him tomorrow. So ignoring everything around him, Asher buried his head in his job and hoped that things would take care of themselves for a change. They wouldn't, but he could hope.

Chapter 6

Zak jumped from the bed and shifted just as he leapt from the window. Jed had no idea what was going on, but fear and other emotions were running all over his body and mind. Lindsey sat up and looked at him, sleep still apparent on her face, and simply said "dragon."

"I know, love, but we'll just go and see what this is about, and both of us will be right back." Nodding, she lay back down, and he smiled. Whatever had woken the two of them up hadn't bothered her, it seemed. Hearing the rest of the house running down the stairs from their bedrooms, Jed pulled on his shirt and the rest of his clothing covered him as he moved to the door.

His pants were on as soon as he opened their door. Shoes covered his feet even as he stepped, socks filled his shoes, and as he made his way down the first landing, he had on a jacket as well as a hat. He was out on the decking with the rest of the others as the dragon parts of them scattered to the sky. It was then that Jed saw them.

"Christ." Yes, he thought that about summed it up. And when Simeon continued, he watched the newcomers as they hovered quietly above the lawn. "Who the hell are they, and where the fuck did they come from?"

Jed felt her before she moved out onto the deck. As he reached for her, Lindsey moved by him and into the yard. Before he could guess her intent, she walked up to the pair of dragons just as they landed with a hard thud on the grass, and put her hand on the snout of the larger of the two. A conversation that was unintelligible to most everyone standing there began between Lindsey and the dragon.

"He said you were expecting him." Jed moved toward her, and she put up her other hand to stop him. "They're afraid of you for now, so please just stay back. And they would very much like it if you were to call the other dragons in. They're being pursued and they do not want anyone to know where they have landed."

In minutes the dragons, their dragons, landed near them. Each of them stayed as they were. Jed figured if anything happened, they'd be able to defend more than they could currently.

"Can they shift or are they in their truest forms?" Asher stepped off the deck, but he only sat on the steps as he talked to Lindsey. He wasn't going to go any closer, but he was establishing who was in charge. Essie stood behind him, and Kiaran on his right. "Can they speak to us too?"

"No. They are in their true form. But he said that he has not been on such magical land before, so does not know if he can be a man or not." Lindsey turned to Asher. "I'd really like to know why I can do this. I mean, while I'm not freaking out—okay, trying not to freak out—I'm standing next to a dragon that is about fifty times bigger than you guys as dragons."

"I'm not sure, and while I'm glad that you're feeling a little freaked out, don't let this bother you overly much. If he was going to harm you, he would have done it by now." Essie smacked Asher on the back of the head before he could continue. "I'm only saying that she's in good hands and we appreciate what she's doing."

"You're scaring her." Essie looked at Jed. "Did you know about this? Or maybe where she might have gotten this power?"

"No. But like Asher, I think she's going to be fine." He really didn't think that, but it was better than scaring Lindsey more. He looked at her now. "Love? Has he told you who they are? Or why they're here?"

"Yes. His name is Silco and hers is Yviene. She is his mate. They're expecting." The big dragon put his palm out, and Lindsey sat down on it. He huffed at the ground and a small flame lit the dry earth. "He's asking that you not be alarmed, but he noticed that I'm cold. I'm starting to like this guy. He's very…not funny, but old world, like Mr. Elbert and Mr. Jacob."

"When is Yviene due?" Essie moved closer, but she didn't touch any of them. "Tell him that I should very much like to touch her, to make sure that she and her hatchling are doing well."

"He said that he knows that she is very tired and that you may…he said that you are his queen. Is that right?" Essie nodded and put her hand on the other dragon's head. "He would like for me to tell him what you say. I don't think he can understand you. Do you understand why I can?"

"No. But I would imagine that he's speaking his language. Dragon. I'm not sure if the others can speak it, but we'll figure that out soon." Essie looked at her as she spoke. "Tell him that his lady wife is doing well and that his hatchling is a male, should he like to know. Also, tell him that there is a cave nearby that they may use until she has bred."

Jed moved off the deck when Asher stood up. He didn't know what was going on either, but Zak moved to come with him. Jed asked Lindsey to tell Silco that they were her mates as well.

"He knows. He said that he could smell you on me." She glared at him and Zak. "You should also know that he said that he thinks you are keeping something from me."

Jed stopped moving, as did Zak. He was keeping something from her—the two of them were—and they had meant to tell her, but she'd distracted them again. As he moved closer again, the dragon lifted his head, but he made no attempt to harm them.

"He's protecting her, so I would tread lightly if I were you. And from now on, you might want to make it a point to tell her everything you know."

Jed nodded at Essie, but didn't take his eyes off the big dragon. "I was going to tell you."

Lindsey nodded and the dragon put his head back down. It was even bigger than it had looked from the porch. He hadn't ever seen a dragon other than the ones that they'd grown up with. "Could you ask him to see if he can shift? He doesn't have to do it now. I know that he must be exhausted, but if he could, that would be wonderful."

"Silco said that if the king and queen are finished, he and his mate will go to rest but will return later this evening. He also said to tell you that while he is being pursued, he does not believe that the person chasing him is all that close." Lindsey turned to Asher. "What could a man do against a dragon this large?"

"I'm not sure, but we'll find out tomorrow. Tell him to rest, but not to go too deeply into the cave. Tell him that it's a resting place for someone that means a great deal to us all, and we should like her not to be disturbed." When Lindsey stood up, Jed took her into his arms. Zak stood next to her as well and touched her with his wing. It was a show of possession and one that he'd never thought he'd use with her, but it felt right. The dragon stood up and bowed before all of them before he put his hand out to Lindsey.

"He wants to give me something for what I've done for them." She looked at Jed, and all he could think about was that she was talking to the dragon and they were no longer touching. "I told him that I've no need for payment, but he said that I have to ask you about it."

"You have to accept it, love. It's a tradition among dragons that dates back for more years that most of us have been around. And I would say that this fellow is older than even us." Jed watched as she moved toward the dragon, who turned his hand over to reveal an old leather sack inside of it. Lindsey picked it up when he nodded. "Tell him that you are his servant and that you thank him and his mate."

When the smaller dragon took to the sky, the larger one bowed to him again. As Jed returned the gesture, the dragon took to the sky to follow his mate. Jed waited until Zak shifted before he spoke to Lindsey. To be honest, he was as terrified as when the thing let her touch him, but he didn't ask to see what she'd been given.

"It's my first gift ever." He asked her what she meant. "I mean, it's my birthday. And I've never gotten anything before. Not that I'm asking for it now, but I only just realized it when he gave this to me."

"Then we should celebrate." She shook her head, but Jed nodded and his mind was going full ahead on things they could do for her today. "We'll leave in an hour. Don't pack anything, and Zak and I will take you out in style."

She protested all the way into the house, but he could feel her excitement as well. As she moved up the stairs, Jed looked at Zak. He was grinning too.

"Our place. We'll take her there and then out to dinner. Somewhere really nice where she has to dress up." Zak looked at him with the most devilish smile on his face. "What else do you have in mind?"

"We'll get her a ring. I'll make the gem for her, but we'll get it made for her while we're in town." Jed loved the idea, and more so since he'd been thinking of a design for days now. He and Zak made their way into the house, but stopped when Grandda asked them to stay.

"She's not human." Jed sat down, and Zak leaned against the counter as Grandda continued. "I have thought…until today I wasn't sure, but I have contacted Caroline and she is on her way. But I am to ask you if you know if she has a mark on her body. It would look like a dragon."

"She's a dragon?" Grandda shook his head and told them that while he wasn't sure what she was, she wasn't a dragon. "Then what?"

"I do not know, but she can talk to dragons. Not just any, but ones that are older than us, as well as fully dragon. That is something that I have never run into before. And as you know, I have been around for a very long time." Grandda was older than them by centuries.

When he moved through the house to the dining room, Jed looked at Zak.

"Do you know?" Zak said that he had no idea. "Not that it changes our plans, but we will have to protect her more. If this person that is after dragons finds out she can…holy shit. She knew."

"Knew what? What is it?" Jed told Zak about the conversation that he'd had with her when the dragons had shown up. "She knew they were out there before we did?"

"I'm thinking that she might have been guiding them here. Remember what Caroline told us? There would be a light that would guide the others to us. I have no idea why I thought it would be Asher or Essie, but it's her. I know it is." He thought of her as their guide. "Zak, if someone finds out she can bring the dragons to her, then whoever is searching for them is going to want her in their clutches. She'll be hurt."

"No, we won't let them. But I think you're right. We'll have to keep her closer to us. At least until we find out for sure."

Jed was already sure but said nothing as they made their way to the bedroom. He told Asher what they were doing, then what he thought of Lindsey. Asher wasn't keen on them leaving with her.

She told us it's her birthday. Zak and I are going to take her out in style. And we'll keep an eye on her. Asher relented, but Jed knew he wasn't happy about it. *If it makes you feel any better, we'll take her to the next town over so that no one knows who she is.*

He and Asher talked about where they were going and how long they were going to be gone as he packed up. They didn't really need much as they were going to stay at his place in the city, but he wanted to have a few things. Zak wasn't going to get to be out while they were gone, but he was excited. And the emerald that he'd given Jed for her ring was the exact color of her eyes. Things were looking perfect for their trip.

~~~

The bag that Silco had given her was still unopened on her lap. Lindsey wanted to open it, but was so excited that it was all hers that she wanted to keep the suspense alive for a little while longer. She had told the men that it was her first birthday gift, but truthfully it was her first gift of any kind from anyone. Not that she didn't enjoy the clothing from Zak and Jed, but this wasn't something that she'd needed.

The drive to the city and to wherever they were taking her was something else that was preoccupying her mind. It was a good thing, too, since she was trying her best not to think about having talked to a giant dragon.

"Do you know if you have a mark on your body that looks like a dragon?" Lindsey looked at Jed. "I'm only asking because I was asked to see if you have one. I've talked to Zak and he said that he doesn't remember seeing one. But he also pointed out that when you're naked around us, we don't think about marks on your body."

Her face heated at all the times these two had been naked with her as well. They were…she was beginning to think there was something wrong with her. All she wanted to do all the time was have one or both of them making love to her. She could not get enough of them. When Jed cleared his throat, she tried to remember what he'd asked her.

"No, I don't think I have a mark on me that looks like a dragon. Or any shape, for that matter. I can't see all of my body, but I've never seen it on the parts that I can see."
~~~

She felt Zak move and she looked at Jed. "I felt him. I mean, I know that Zak is on your back and near your neck. Is that right?"

"Yes. He wants to pull free of me to touch you but he can't, not without being on the homeland. I don't know a lot about the magic there, but it's the only place that the dragons can be both human and dragon." She started to say something but thought he'd think her stupid. "What is it? Tell me."

"I'm thinking that he doesn't have to just be a part of you anymore. I don't know why, but…well, I think he could separate from you and be with us while we're together." Again, she had no idea why she thought that, but she was reasonably sure it was true. "Can he try? I mean, will it distract you from driving?"

Jed pulled the big truck over and pulled off his shirt. She wanted to touch him, run her hands over the dragon that had moved to his chest, but she knew that once she did, they'd not be going anywhere for a while.

"Touch us." His voice made her think of his voice when he came or when he was commanding her to come. Putting her hand on Zak's head, she felt him on Jed's body and ran her hand down along his neck to his wings. "Tell him, Lindsey. Call to Zak and see if he can be separate from me."

"Come to me, Zak."

He moved against her hand, and she felt her breath catch. He was pulling from Jed. His dragon was moving from Jed's body to move over hers physically. When he had her laid back over the seat, his naked body rocking into hers, she felt Jed pull her legs apart as he told her to undress.

Naked now, Jed slid his fingers into her pussy and she rode him. Zak, his human body now sitting on the floorboard, was suckling at her breasts and pulling hard on her nipples. She was so close to coming that she curled her fingers in his hair to hold him to her as she watched Jed fuck her with his fingers.

"I'd like nothing more than to take you on my lap and let you fuck me." Suddenly, she found herself in Jed's lap and Zak sitting by her. When she was lifted up, Jed moved to the center of the seat and sucked her breasts while she was moved around to face him. Coming down on his cock had her moaning, especially as she watched Zak fist himself.

"When he comes in you, I'm going to pull you down on me to take my share of you." Nodding, she watched Zak's cock get wetter and wetter and licked her lips. "If you keep looking at me like that, love, I'm going to come all over the two of you."

"Yes." She rode Jed, who was feasting on her breasts like he was a starved man. When she moved closer to him, her clit touching his hard belly just above his cock, Zak leaned back on the seat and she wrapped her hand around him. "Come for me, Jed. Come now."

Even as her body exploded around Jed, she felt his hands dig deep into her hips, holding her hard against him as he came with her. Looking at her mate, Zak still held his cock, and as soon as Jed let her go, she pulled her hand from Zak's cock and leaned over him, while still astride Jed, and took Zak into her mouth. In seconds he was coming too, his body nearly up off the seat as he held her mouth over him.

His cum was hot, and he fucked her mouth hard. Jed pressed hard against her clit and she came again, screaming out her release around Zak's cock. Jed was fucking her again with his fingers, hard and fast, while she sucked Zak's cock, and she felt her body gearing up for another climax. This time when she was moved, it was to sit on Zak's cock while he still sat over the seat.

Her body was touched both in the front by Zak and behind by Jed. He lifted her breasts for Zak to taste. He pulled at her nipples hard as he rolled them in his fingers. Zak helped her rock over him, his hands pulling her up and down as she rode him. When teeth grazed her neck, Lindsey leaned her head to the side to give Jed whatever he needed, and when he bit her, his cum splashed against her back as he came. Zak, biting into her breast, had her holding onto him because she knew that she was close to coming apart. When he sucked hard at her nipple, Lindsey screamed as the world around her seemed to just blink out.

When she woke, Lindsey found herself being cradled in Zak's arms as Jed drove the car. As she sat up Jed winked at her, and she felt her body heat up again. It really didn't take much for her to want them again, and that embarrassed her slightly. After she pulled on clothing, she sat between Jed and Zak and tried to think of something to say. It was Zak that helped her out.

"You have a mark. We found it while you were napping." Her face heated more. "You look so adorable when you're embarrassed. But as for the mark, it's under your arm, here."

He showed her the mark. It was indeed under her left arm and had so much detail, it looked like someone had printed it on her. The rearview mirror was adjusted so she could get a better look at it, and she wondered how long it had been there.

"We've never seen it before now." She told Jed she'd not seen it either. "Then we can only assume that you got it when we all came together, or when you were in the cave. I don't know if anyone told you or not, but we found you in the cave that Zak's mother died in. I'm pretty sure that she's given you this ability."

"I think I heard her." Lindsey tried to remember what she'd said. "Something about a gift. She said for me to take it."

"My mom." She looked at Zak. "I think she was giving you the ability to talk to the dragons so that we could help them. We were told that there were more coming. And we're pretty sure that you're guiding them here. We have to keep you safer now. Anyone that finds out about this talent of yours will take you to bring the dragons to them through you. Including us."

"So now I can talk to and understand the other dragons. Do you think they'll all be as nice as the one that came today with his mate?" Neither of them knew. "More than likely not. It's been my experience that people—and I would think dragons are within that group—are only nice when they want something. You and your family are the exception to that rule, but I bet that not many more are."

"So long as you're with us, we'll make sure that you are treated well and that you have all that you need." Lindsey thought of her dreams of lots of hot food and a warm bed, and realized she had more than she'd ever had in her life. Actually, more than she had ever dreamed of having with the love of these two.

"I really don't care if people are nice or good to me. I have all I need and then some. And if I have to kick some ass, I really think I could do that now. All by myself." She looked at Jed when he laughed. "You don't think I can?"

"I was thinking that if Cox were to try and take you now, the man would shit himself. You are not the same person you were a few days ago. And in a few more, you're going to be amazing, more so than you are right now." Thinking it was a strange compliment, she accepted it anyway. Looking at Zak, she realized he was laughing, too, and then pulled her to him and kissed her.

"I don't care if you can or can't kick ass. Today is the first day in my whole life that I'm going to the city as a man, and you did that for me. I will be your slave for the rest of my life." He pulled her onto his lap again and rocked upward, his hard cock pressing against her ass. "And if you let me fuck you while we're here, I'll happily die a sated man."

"You two are the best thing that has ever happened to me. And getting to be fucked by you two makes my life complete." Lindsey stretched, making sure that her ass pressed against him while she did so. "And if you make me come a lot while we're here, I might join you in the afterlife as a sated woman."

"Christ, how soon before we get to your house?" Zak cupped her pussy. "I could bring you now and you'd be able to wait, right?"

She didn't care how many times they brought her, she was never going to get enough, she thought. As he played with her pussy, bringing her close to the edge, then backing off, she knew as soon as they got to where they were going she was going to make him pay. Make them both pay.

Picking up her gift, she opened it and looked at the things inside. Zak offered his lap up as a table, and she poured it out. Not only were there about a dozen gems (she'd bet anything they were diamonds), but also a small scale that she was sure must be a part of the big dragon. Her body heated again as soon as she held it in her hand, and she felt a need so powerful that she had Jed not just pull over, but drive deep into the woods. She needed to be fucked right now. Almost as soon as he turned off the truck, she was pulling at her clothing. And the moment she was naked, Lindsey begged—no, *commanded*—them to fuck her. Nothing else mattered but them and their cocks. Lindsey thought that something was seriously wrong with her as she screamed out her release. Very seriously wrong with her.

Chapter 7

Brandon tried to keep his story straight. He'd been surprised to find the car in the drive when he'd come back from his errands, and more so when the big man stepped in front of him when he started to turn around and run off until whoever it was left. Instead he found himself standing in the hot sun answering questions that he didn't want to answer.

"So you knew that you had to pay a stipend each year, but you refused to pay it." Brandon nodded, then shook his head. "Which is it, Mr. Cox? Yes or no? Did you know about the payment? And you refused to pay it?"

"I knew about the money, but I never had it to spare. I knew about it, but didn't refuse to pay it. There is a difference, you know." The man told him again how much he would have had to save a week to make the payment. "I didn't have the ten cents. I just told you that."

"You didn't have ten cents to put back, yet here you are with an empty fifty-two inch plasma television box in front of your house. And that box? It looks brand new, Mr. Cox." Brandon looked down the road at the box. He'd used one of the credit cards that was in his stash, but didn't think the man would appreciate knowing where he got the money. "Not to mention, it looks to me like you have on a new shirt and pants too. The tags are still on them."

"It was on sale." Lame. Lame. Lame. He knew that even before the man started to laugh. As he jerked off the tags of the new clothing, he felt his temper spin out of control. "You have no right to be on my property. I would very much like for you to leave me alone and not return."

"Can't do that. I have to serve you." Now this sounded more like it. But when he was shoved an envelope at his chest, Brandon had no choice but to take it. "Mr. Cox, you have thirty days to leave the premises. And if you are not vacated at the end of that time, the police will come in and remove you. And if they do, your television will be taken as collateral."

"Collateral for what?" The man just laughed at him as he made his way back to his car. "I asked you a question. What does my television have to do with this?"

"You are, as of this month, fifty dollars behind. And because of the interest, you have amassed a grand total of sixty dollars in back payments. The owners of the property have decided that there will be no more extensions, and as of now, you are to vacate for nonpayment." Brandon asked if he could pay him the money. "No, I'm sorry, sir, you are out of time. Even if you did have the money, which you have said to me several times that you do not, I'm not going to be able to take it. As I have said, they have decided to take the option of having you removed rather than have you try to pay them what you owe. You have a good day now."

As he drove off, Brandon stood there with the envelope in his hand. *What the hell am I supposed to do now*?

he asked himself. Not only did he have no place to go if they kicked him out of his house, but he had no money or transportation to get there even if he knew where to go. He looked at the smoke curling out of the house that he knew the owners lived in. This wasn't a way to treat the people who depended on the land for their livelihood. And he had, all these years, depended greatly on it. Not just for his livelihood, like food and a house, but for his entertainment as well. This was just not fair.

While he was contemplating how to get to the house to talk to the people living there, a car pulled up behind him and he turned to see yet another man getting out of a nice car.

"Mr. Cox?" He nodded, having nowhere to run now that the man had seen him. And even if he did, the gun on the man's hip sort of made him a little nervous. "I'm here about your mother, Maxine Cox. There is a matter of her unpaid bills."

"She's broke." The man came toward him, and Brandon backed up. When he hit the cruiser that had been in the yard for the last five years or so, he nearly fell on his ass. "My mother is in that home that doesn't cost me nothing. The taxes that I pay are supposed to take care of that. But.... Wait a second there. How did you find out who she was, anyway?"

The man only smiled at him, and Brandon felt his butt tighten up. There was something very scary about that smile. And the fact that it didn't get anywhere near his eyes gave him a chilling feeling that went all the way to his toes. When the man pulled something from his side where the gun was hanging, Brandon closed his eyes, knowing that he was going to be shot.

"Here." He took the second envelope and held it to his chest, watching the man. "You've been served. Have a good day."

"Have a good day? How the hell am I supposed to have…? That other man said I can't live here anymore, and now you come here telling me that there is money owed by my mother? She's not worth anything. Don't you know that? It's why I stuffed her in that place in the first place. And even if I did have the money to pay for her to be there, what the hell did she have to spend money on anyway? You guys were supposed to keep her fed and cared for." At least he thought they were.

"She's had expenses that you are still required to cover. The walker to use when she was getting around. Then there was the extra for her wash to be done for her. Those things are not included in the state fees. Not to mention her updated clothing and shoes. All those were to be provided by you, her only living relative." The man opened his car door, but stood there watching him before just shaking his head before he continued. "You just put your mother in that place without any kind of support, and haven't gone to see her in all these years, have you? Not to mention, you've never sent her a card for her birthday, or even for any holidays. What is wrong with you? She's your mother, for Christ's sake."

"I've been busy." He hadn't and he was pretty sure that man knew that. "I don't have time to run in to see her every time she wants her feet rubbed. And cards cost money. It's not like she knew who I was anyway. She's out of her mind."

It had taken him almost a full year after she'd left to get the smell of her feet off his hands. His dad had done rubbed them sometimes—to give him a break, he'd told him—but Brandon had been the one to keep the bedsores off her feet by rubbing them. That was another reason he'd put her in the home. To just get away from her smelly feet.

"Well, Mr. Cox, you won't have to make a trip now. I'm sorry to be the one to tell you this, but she died last week." He got into his car and rolled down the window to tell him the rest. "And as for her not knowing anything, she was pretty lively, they told me. Dancing and singing when the mood struck her. Even going so far as to help the gardeners out when the flowers were planted. She told the administrators what her name was, as well as how to reach you a few days before she died. I think she might have been a little pissed with you for your lack of niceties. You're a real piece of work."

His mom was lively? Not so long as he knew her. And as far as Brandon could remember, she couldn't sing anything other than those country songs. Used to drive his daddy crazy the way she'd twang around the house.

"I'm not paying these bills. I got no money, you hear me? None." The man simply started his car and backed out of the drive. Almost as soon as he was on the road, another car pulled in. "Mother fuck. Go away. If you want something, I don't have it. It's all gone."

By the time this man left, telling him that he was to come to the courthouse and talk to them about missing women, Brandon was shaking so hard that he hurt from it. He knew as surely as he was standing there that Lindsey had given him up. There certainly couldn't have been nobody else, as they were all dead and most of them were currently wrapped in traps in one of the caves. Putting them there instead of burying them had saved him a lot of work, but dragging them behind the four-wheeler that he'd stolen a few years ago had made it a lot easier. He wondered briefly if the people at the big house had noticed that the big machine was gone yet.

As soon as he was sure that he wasn't going to have any more unwelcome visitors, he went in the house and locked the doors. Laying all the paperwork he'd been given on the table, he looked around the house. It was dirty again...beyond that, it really stank too. And Lindsey had only been gone for a couple of weeks. As soon as the next woman came to his house, she was going to have to see what she was going to have to work with by having to clean up after him. She'd have her work cut out for her, that was for sure. He didn't have the energy to deal with this and the visitors too. It had been a terrible day and he didn't even have his television hooked up. And he needed that nice piece of equipment more than ever now. Something to take his mind off his miseries.

Deciding that he was going to walk over to the big house tomorrow, Brandon pulled the television to his stand. It was a lot bigger than he'd thought it had been in the ad, and the guy who had brought it out to him had asked if he needed help setting it up. Brandon said he'd do it, and the man just shrugged and took off. He'd not even helped him get it into the house. Now, as he was reading the instructions, Brandon realized how complicated the thing was. Nothing was working out for him today at all.

He didn't have any cable wires. Not that he had cable, but the instructions were very specific about having those wires put in the plugs on the television. Not sure what to do, he put one of the phone chargers in the place of the cable and decided it would have to do. Then it was time for him to hook up the Internet so he could download movies. That was another problem, and not one that he could figure out how to work either.

It sounded like a really good idea. There was even a coupon for his first rental. Again, he wasn't sure how that was supposed to work, but he put some more of the chargers in the place of the Internet cables, having to tape a few of them so they'd stay in place, and plugged the electricity into the television. When nothing happened, he pulled all the wires out and started again.

It was nearly midnight when he went to bed. The house was freezing again, and he'd not gotten to watch a single thing on his new television. There had been a great deal of static, but other than that, nothing. He'd had to start over so many times and put all the things back in the same place that he'd lost count. And no matter what he did, nothing would work the way the instructions said they would.

He tried to sleep, but he was so mad that all he wanted to do was go to the living room and bash the television to pieces. But he was tired, and when he was tired he was cranky too. He knew this so stayed where he was so that he'd not ruin his television. He knew that he could get it to work, but had been too upset to do so just now. So he rolled in the blankets and willed himself to sleep.

Getting up late the next morning, he ignored the television for breakfast. Then when he realized just how late it really was, he dressed in his finest new clothing and set out for the big house. He had his paperwork with him. He hadn't had time to search out the original contract that was older than anything he knew of, but he had the envelopes that he'd been given yesterday. He wasn't sure what the people could do about his mom and stuff, but this other thing he knew they'd fix once they heard his story. And he had a good one too. He was still working on what to do about the missing women, but telling them that he was out of work, had no money, and that he'd not been able to pay, Brandon knew that he'd be able to get off without any trouble whatsoever, and he'd at least have a home to stay in until he could figure it out.

As soon as he made it to the clearing, he knew that he should have brought him a clean shirt. The one he had on was soaked through with his sweat, and it stank. There were stains all the way down the sides to his pants, and they were dirty too. Falling several times when he'd tried to get over some fallen logs, he had mussed himself up pretty good.

He saw a woman in a field of what appeared to be nothing more than wet grass, then he saw her filling a basket with weeds. Off her rocker, he thought. Collecting weeds was just plain dumb.

After waving several times, he waited for her to come to him when she finally did see him. Looking around the field, he was envious of the new truck that was just pulling into the yard behind the house, and there was a car that looked as big as his house too. Flowers everywhere seemed to brighten up the darkest corners of the deep forest, as well as the big wrap-around porch. Not just in the big pots that sat on it, but in the yard too. He wanted to ask her about that, but he needed to talk to them first. Waving again, he was surprised when a big dog came around the side of the tree he was near and growled at him.

"Nice dog." The dog didn't appear to know that he wasn't there to harm him and came closer to Brandon, with his hair standing up and his teeth, big sharp ones, showing. As Brandon backed away from him, he heard someone laugh and looked to his right to see the woman. She was pretty, but he didn't care for her laughter. Especially when he knew she was laughing at him.

"Can I help you before he tears you apart?" Brandon looked at the dog again and noticed that he'd halved the distance between them. "I asked you a question, Mr. Cox. What can I help you with?"

"You know me?" The woman said nothing but stared at him with a strange smile. "I come to talk to the men of the house. You can go and get one of them for me."

"Oh? And you think they can help you better than I can?" He wasn't sure what she was asking him, so he told her that men knew a great deal. "I'm sure they do, but in this case, you'll talk to me or no one. Or you can get your butt back to your house and wait for them to foreclose on you."

"They discussed this with you?" She nodded and moved closer to the dog and put her hand on his head. Brandon had an urge to hit her, but the dog growled against her so he didn't as much as move his hands. "I need to talk to them. I have me a problem that I want to discuss with a man. I have been served. They said I have to move out of my house, and I don't think that's very fair of them."

"I'm well aware that you've been served. Several times, as a matter of fact." He didn't like her knowing his business and told her that. "Too bad for you then. I won't help you, so you might as well go on back home and await your fate."

"You can't help me? But you just said that you were all I could talk to." She said that she wouldn't help him, not that she couldn't. Not that he understood the difference, but he wasn't happy with it all the same. "I don't want to lose my home. It's been in my family for a long time, and it's not right that I have to move out. I don't have anyone else. My momma died and I'm gonna have to bury her."

"She died over a week ago, and she's already buried in the county cemetery. And so you know, I also am aware of the summons you received for her outstanding bills. Have you any idea how you're planning to pay that ten grand?" He staggered back at the amount…surely she had that wrong. "You didn't read the paperwork you were given, did you? Not only do you owe the housing department for her necessities, but you also have to pay for her burial and anything else associated with her death. You are in debt for a great deal of money, Mr. Cox. However will you pay it?"

"I didn't have time to read over that stuff, and if they think that I'm going to pay for her necessities when I don't have any of my own, then they're nuttier than she is…was." He'd been too busy with his new television. "You can't have that right. That's why I insist on speaking to a man. You don't know what you're talking about."

The dog moved closer to him and snapped his teeth at his hand that hadn't moved so much as an inch. Brandon jumped back so quickly that he fell on his butt, and scrambled back more when the dog seemed to leap at him. The woman laughed at him again and he wanted to put her in her place, but he didn't move. The dog was sure to eat him alive if he did. He heard someone coming up behind him just as he started to stand again. This was just stupid.

"What's going on?" Brandon knew that voice and turned to see her. "Hello, Brandon. Have you killed any women lately? Or are you thinking that I'm going to come back and *work* for you again? Either way, it's not going to happen. Not ever again."

~~~

Lindsey was afraid. Not that there weren't enough people around her to help her out, but he would know where she was now, and she had a feeling that he'd come back and hurt her or someone that lived here. As he lay there and stared at her, all she could think about were the boxes in his attic.

Zak, Jed, and herself had just gotten home, and she saw Essie out in the field and had decided to go and tell her what a great time they'd had. And to show her the bracelet she'd gotten. She was about halfway to her when she saw the man, and Elbert in his other form too.

"You make it sound as though you were not well paid for your duties to me." Lindsey only laughed, which seemed to piss him off more, and that made her day. "You will not take that tone with me, young lady. You are to come back to the house right now and begin your duties. I have some things to go over with you as well. Rules that you're going to follow from now on."

He actually thought she was going to do as he said. And when he stood, the big dog sat down and cocked his head at her as if he was asking her, "Are you going to put up with this shit?"

"I'm not going back there where you can chain me to the floor and beat me when you think I've done something wrong. And I don't know what sort of payment you think you gave me, but I didn't get shit from you. Nothing but grief and terror the entire time I was there." Lindsey felt Jed and Zak come up behind her and felt braver for it. Neither one touched her, but she knew that they were
~~~

there for support should she need it. "Where is Donna or Shelly? Or any of the other women whose things you have in your attic?"

He paled, and then he jumped up off the ground. Taking a step back, she felt the tattoo on her arm, the one that had gotten bigger since she'd noticed it yesterday, start to burn. As she backed from Brandon again she was careful where she was, not wanting to trip over anything and give him any excuse to hurt her. When he was standing up and about four or so feet from her, Lindsey stood very still, thinking that was a better idea.

"You have no right to be in my things." He stepped to her again. "You will come back with me this minute, or so help me I will tell everyone what I know about you."

"They know." That stopped him for all of a second. Not glancing at either of the men or Essie, she thought about all that she'd *not* told them. And it hurt her. Lifting her chin, she felt the earth under her feet start to move. Not much, but enough to let her know that something was going on. Essie must have been helping her, she thought, and she glared at Brandon.

It was then that the gun suddenly appeared in his hand. It took her several seconds to realize that he was going to shoot her, and more than likely the people with her as well. It had never occurred to her that he'd kill her, or even try. He'd been hurtful to her and mean, but never murderous.

"You'll do as I say right now or so help me, I'll kill you all where you stand. I've had a really bad couple of days, and I just can't take any more." She nodded and put her hands behind her back. The mark on her arm, the sigil, as Zak had called it, was not just burning now, but felt like it was going to take her arm off. Zak was talking and Jed was touching her arms, but she could only focus on the gun and that it was pointed at her. "Come with me now, Lindsey, and this will be just a bad dream."

The ground now shook her off her feet. Even as she started to fall, her body seemingly floating to the earth, a great wind took her breath away and she felt herself being lifted up off the ground. Watching the scene below her as if she were not a part of it, Lindsey watched the man that had tormented her for so long run, firing the gun over his shoulder as he went.

Nothing was making sense. There were bright colors that had not been there before, reds and dark stains. Essie was moving in a way that made Lindsey think that she, too, was rising up from the earth, but that wasn't even close to being possible. *Right*? she asked herself.

Even as the earth trembled again, shaking the great trees that she moved over, the sky darkened and the sun blotted out. Looking upward, Lindsey had a moment of fear at what she was seeing, but her mind seemed to just take it all in. Everything, it seemed, was all right. She was going to be just fine.

Landing on her feet, she looked at the dragon in front of her. Zak. Someone she knew. And as she wrapped her arms around him, his wings, strong and warm, wrapped around her and held her to him. Nothing would harm her here. No one could shoot her while she was being held. Holding him tightly, thinking of what she'd seen, then letting her mind blank out again, she started to cry. And when it was too much for her body, she let it go as well.

Hands were touching her. She knew on some level that she'd been hurt, but was not sure how. The pain in her belly was making her a little light-headed, and the voices, all of them shouting at her, were making her head swirl around. Looking into the face that seemed to be so close, she recognized her on some level but was not really sure from where.

Don't die on me. I need you to breathe. Nodding, she tried to do that, but nothing seemed to be working. *Come on, damn it, just breathe. They need you.*

Nodding again, she felt her breath seem to whoosh out of her. The woman smiled, then turned to look around. She did as well and noticed that everyone was sleeping, and Lindsey wondered if the woman was doing that.

Lindsey attempted to sit up but didn't have the strength. The woman looked at her again. When she smiled, so did Lindsey, and when she moved around the room, touching the men there, she realized that she could see right through her.

I'm not really here, as you have guessed. I am still below the earth, lying just where I took my last breath so very long ago. Feeling like a simpleton after nodding again, Lindsey saw the woman smiling at her as she continued. *You're just fine now. The bullet did not harm you overly much. And now that I have helped you, you will never feel things like that again.*

"Who are you?" The woman looked at her as she drifted toward her. "How did I get hurt and where...? Something happened."

It did. But you are well, so you will not have to worry again. The woman moved to touch her, and despite her telling Lindsey that she wasn't in the room with her, she could feel it. The touch was warm. *You call to them, our kind. It was all that saved you. And when you called to them, you called to me as well. And my mate. I can feel him now when I could not before.*

"You're the dragon queen." The smile was breathtaking, and Lindsey was warmed by that as well.

"Will they be able to see you, too? I know that they miss you very much."

Nay, I do not think so. But I should like for you to tell them that I love them very much. Lindsey told her that she would. *Also, I have a favor to ask. There is a demon below the ground at the castle keep. Should you go there, you will be able to call him forth, but you should only do so when the moon is full and with all of the men and their other halves with you. Nary a one can be missing. Understand?*

"I do. But how do I summon a demon? And once he's there, what the heck do I do with him then?" The queen told her to ask Elbert, he'd have the information. "Will he also know what I'm supposed to do with him once I get him out of the ground?"

Ask Elbert. I promise you, if he does not know the answer to your questions, then he will find them for you. Caroline will know as well. Have you met the white witch? Lindsey told her that she didn't think so. *You have not then. But my sons, all of them, they know her. And they will be there with you.*

"They love being at the castle and doing what they're doing to bring it back. They want to bring it back to life." The queen nodded and moved to touch her fingers to Zak's head, then his arm. As she did the same to Jed, Lindsey spoke again, "They're my mates."

They are. And fine men they turned out to be. I have shared with them what I have given you, my child. I have seen Essie and Asher, too. She is very strong and will do nicely as the queen. The woman turned to her again. *Remember. Nary a one can be missing when you call to him. All twelve of them must be there.*

As she disappeared, Lindsey felt herself drifting away. That was when the nightmarish scenes came to show themselves, and she drifted further into her sleep to hide from them.

Chapter 8

Jed watched her while he sat on the big porch. It had been three days since she'd woken up, and not only had she not said a single word to anyone, she'd stopped eating as well. They were all worried about her, he most of all. Late at night when everyone was sleeping, he heard her speaking.

"We might have to take her to the hospital soon if she doesn't eat. And Silco has not left the yard since he showed up to save her life." Jed only nodded at Zak. He was worried as well, he knew. "I heard her last night."

"Me too. She's been talking out of her head, don't you think?" Zak said nothing, and Jed looked at him. "She didn't see all that, did she, Zak? I mean, you took her away before Silco got here."

"I don't know for sure. But from what she's talking about at night, I'd say she saw a great deal more than we did. And who is she talking about when she says twelve men? Us?" Jed told him he thought so. "Then what are we to do? And who is she going to bring here that she fears so much?"

Jed told him that he had no idea unless it was Silco. But now that he'd been thinking it over, he thought it wasn't him, but maybe someone else. Instead of dwelling on something he couldn't figure out, he thought about the day that Silco had come to her. And now, both he and Zak could talk to him as well.

"She called to me." Jed had already figured that part out when Silco spoke to him. "She was in danger and she needed me like none other had before."

"You saved her. There would have been no way for us to get her to safety had you not stepped in to kill that man." He'd bitten him in half and then burned him to nothing with his flame. And a great flame it had been. Only seconds of it had not just burned the man, but there were no traces of him to bury either. The ground was still scorched from it. Nothing would go near it, including them.

"She needed me and I had no choice but to help her." Jed thanked him again, as had the rest of the family. "I shall await her here, if you have no care of it. There is still danger about, but I do not believe that it will harm her now. Not with so many coming."

"Coming? More dragons?" Asher looked at Jed when Silco answered him. "More dragons coming is going to be difficult to keep hidden. If anyone finds any of us here, there will be hell to pay."

"The castle will hide us." Asher asked Silco what he meant. "I know not, my king. Only that the castle, even in the state that it is in, holds more power than any of us have seen in centuries. It is as if it holds it just for you."

Jed still had no idea what that had meant. He had tried working it out, even going to the point of writing the entire conversation down so that he could read it over and over to see what he might have missed. But without Lindsey there talking to them and helping them, he didn't have any idea.

"I was going to town. Her ring is ready." Jed looked at Zak, who had also lost some weight. "I want to get it for her."

"That's a good idea. And can you pick up some of those chocolate éclairs that she loved when we took her out to dinner? Maybe it will tempt her to eat." Zak said that he would. As he looked at her, Jed felt his heart hurt for them all. "She'll get better. I know it."

"I think she will as well. But I miss her. Her laughter and her smile. All she does is just sit there, staring out the window like she's waiting for something." Jed pulled a blanket up and over her lap that had fallen. "Let me know if there is any change. As much as I hate to leave her, I need to get away for a minute or two. Just to clear my head."

"I understand." Jed did too. It was hard to just watch her waste away. And after Zak left, he started talking to her again. "I've decided to build us a house. Not a huge one. Only about five bedrooms. And each of them will have a large bed in it so that we can break it in."

He wasn't really going to do that, but he wanted to try and get a rise out of her. The house, however, was being built. As much as he loved living here with his family, it was too close. And he wanted Lindsey to have her own space. This house was Essie's, and two women in the house was going to cause issues. At least he thought so.

Jed was just drifting off when he heard Lindsey speak. He didn't move, just sat there quietly, thinking that she was dreaming again. When she continued to talk, he sat up and listened better.

"I was in jail for a time. Thirty days to be exact. They said that I was a part of three people that robbed a shop in the mall. I didn't even know the other two men." Jed knew this, or at least that she'd been in jail. The rest he had figured out on his own. "Jail kept me out of trouble, I guess. And fed. Even warm for a time. Of course, it felt colder after being warm when I was tossed out on the streets again. But I never did what they said I did. That's why I find it hard to get a job. I have a record."

"I'm having things looked into to have them taken off your record. Not that it matters to me what you've done. I still love you." Her nod had him sitting up higher in his chair as he watched her. "Are you hungry?"

"There was…the queen came to see me." He started to tell her that all of them had been to see her at one point over the last few days, but she continued. "She was here, but not. She told me that I was going to be fine and that I had to summon the great monster in the castle keep. There was more, but I don't remember it right now."

"You mean Essie." She shook her head, and he felt his skin sort of inch along his skin. "The dragon queen? You saw her?"

"Yes." She stared out the window still. Her voice, like his, was soft and low. "She said that she helped me. That I'd not feel the pain of the gunshot wound again. I think…I have been thinking, and I think she gave me a little more than that."

"Like what?" He knew that he and Zak had the same mark as she did. The dragon on her arm was now on theirs in the same place. He supposed that it was why they could talk to the dragons as well, but he did wonder if they could call to them should they need it. "Lindsey, what else do you think she gave you?"

"I don't know really. I have an idea, but not really what it might be." He asked her again what it was. "She said something about making me like her. But that doesn't seem right. Something was off. I'm not sure what it was, but I just feel she was lying to me."

Jed stood up and made his way to her. Sitting on the floor in front of her, he took her hands into his and felt the warmth of them. When she didn't look at him, Jed said her name until she did. It was then that he noticed the darkness of her eyes. They were no longer just green, but a dark, almost black green.

"I love you." She nodded once and started to look away. "Don't, Lindsey; look at me, please. I want to talk to you about what happened that day."

"He was going to shoot me. I guess he did, but he'd been killed before he could finish the job." Jed said nothing but watched her. "The dragon, Silco, he killed him for me. I will need to see about thanking him properly for it."

"You know how to thank a dragon properly?" She nodded and pulled her hand free of his and turned it over. He watched as a small dragon appeared there. It wasn't a real one, but a small version of one that looked like Silco. "Is that an image of his child?"

"It is. He will have a great son and he will, like the others that come, have more than they have ever had before. Mostly it is only safety that they wish, but when they come here, the ability to breed and have strong hatchlings will make it so that their children will not pass too soon. That is his greatest fear. That his child will die before he has a chance to live." As he watched the child's image move, all he could think about was this was his mate and she was far more superior than he'd thought of her being.

"What is it you have to do, Lindsey? What kind of magic do you hold that will make it so that his child and others are born to live?" She looked at him, and the smile made him think of all the times before this that he'd seen it. The way she'd looked so beautiful even when she'd been so terrified. "You are evolving, aren't you?"

"We all are. The three of us are going to be great." He asked her how she knew this. "I don't have any idea, but we are going to help all the dragons that come to us. And there will be more. And when they arrive, they will help us in ways that you guys have never dreamed of. As soon as we get rid of the monster below the ground."

~~~

Zak moved to the bedroom, trying to be as quiet as he could. He'd been so happy to hear from Jed that he'd come right back, and had just barely remembered to get the ring. Now it was late, much later than he wanted to be getting home, but he was home and that was all that mattered. As soon as he stripped off his clothing, Zak slipped into the bed.

"You're cold." Lindsey rolled to him and wrapped her body around his. His cock, never sated as far as she was concerned, seemed to stretch tighter and ache to fill her. "I want you."

"Christ, I want you too." She rolled over him, her nude body highlighted in the moonlight, and he sat up and took her breast into his mouth and bit down hard enough to make her moan. "Ride me. I've missed having you take your pleasure from me."

Helping her to get up on her knees, Zak felt Jed move, but he never joined them. He was grateful for that,
~~~

needing to have her all to himself for now. When she lowered herself over him, taking him deeply, Zak sat up and held her body to his.

Her breasts were lifted by her small hands, and he took the offering as she rode him. He wanted to hold off coming, to take as much of her as he could, but every time she held him to her, moaned out her own pleasure, Zak could feel himself being drawn deeper in and deeper into her spell. When he rolled her to her back and her legs wrapped tightly around him, Zak looked into her eyes as he took her hard, pounded as deep and as hard as he could while watching the pleasure flitter across her face.

"Come in me. Fill me." He had no doubt that he would, but he wanted her to come first. "Please, Zak. Come in me. I want to feel you come deep inside of me."

He felt his balls tighten to his body and his cock fill to the tip as he leaned down and took her mouth. As he kissed her, fucking her mouth with his tongue as he was her body, Lindsey dug her nails deep into his muscle, sending blood trailing down his back. His vision blurred slightly as he felt his entire body burn with the need to come. And when he did let it go, seemingly let the climax rule him, Zak cried out his release, his throat raw with it even as he felt his balls fill again.

Her body bowed up. He watched as she seemed to come apart right before his eyes as she screamed out her own release. Zak fucked her and continued to empty his cock in her over and over. When he dropped over her, his body nearly too weak to move, Jed moved him to his side of the bed and lifted Lindsey up and turned her so that her ass was on the edge of the bed and he behind her.

"Suck his cock while I watch you." She moved her body, already filled with Jed from behind, as he commanded her to take Zak into her mouth. Zak wasn't sure he could take much more, his body spent, but when she wrapped her hand around him, her mouth covering his crown, he roared out, his release nearly taking his breath away.

Her mouth was as hot as she'd been, just as tight too, and he found his body ready and more than willing to fuck her this way. As she moaned around his cock, Zak looked up at Jed as he fucked her pussy, his hands gripping her hips tightly. His face was beautiful, his body covered in a fine sheen of sweat that seemed to sparkle in the moonlight. And when he came, his body bowed back and his hands holding her, he could see every line of his muscles, every vein that filled his heart with blood as he came crying out their name. And Zak fell in love with his other half. Jed had been a part of him for so long, forever, that he'd never thought of being in love with him, but in that moment, he knew that he'd always been. And that Lindsey had brought them together.

None of them moved. Jed stood behind Lindsey, his cock still buried deep within her as he held her gently now, his cheeks expanding hard and quick as he tried to catch his breath. Lindsey lay her head on Zak's belly, her hand still wrapped around him as she licked him clean. It was nearly too much, but he didn't stop her as he thought of all the things that he wanted to say to them. How he wanted to tell them how very much he loved them both. Jed looked at him as he moved, his cock still stiff and covered in Lindsey. Zak moved on the bed, making room for the two people that meant the world to him, and curled around Lindsey when she moved beside him.

Lying there, his body finally calm enough to relax enough to sleep, he looked over at Jed when he moved to hold his head up with his hand, his elbow bent over her pillow. His grin told him that he thought he knew what he'd been thinking.

"She said that she wanted to wait for you." Zak nodded and looked into her sleeping face. "I love you, Zak. I hope you know that."

"I love you as well. I don't think I've said that to you before." Jed said that he'd not either, and now he knew that he'd meant it. "I was thinking that as well. That even though we've been together forever, it has only just occurred to me how much I love you. And her."

"She is amazing, and has taught me so much about life in general." Jed laughed quietly, as low as they'd been speaking. "She wants to have our child. I told her that I had no idea how that worked, but she thinks we can both impregnate her. I'm willing to give it a try. How about you?"

"Yes." He looked into her face again. "She'll be a great mother and wife to us. More than we deserve, I think."

"I think that you're right. But don't tell her that. She gets a might pissy when I say things like that to her." Zak believed him. She didn't take compliments well. "Tomorrow we'll have to talk to Asher. She told me that she's talked to your mom. She said that she has given her magic. I think she might have."

Zak didn't doubt that either. There was something more about Lindsey than there had been before. And if he really thought about it, which he'd not done very much of lately, he thought that perhaps he and Jed both had changed as well. And they were most assuredly stronger than they had been. Then he thought of the conversation they'd had with the attorney that they'd had looking into some of the things that they'd found out about Lindsey.

"Her parents aren't dead as she'd told you. They're not even aware that their daughter is alive. I found them about three days ago, and according to their attorney, they have never given up hope of finding her, even after all this time." Zak asked him what he'd told them about her. "Nothing. Not until I heard from you. And their attorney has promised to get me all he can. I would like to do a DNA test if you don't mind."

"I'll ask her. Why was she put in an orphanage if she wasn't an orphan? Do you know that?" Jed said that he had no idea, but she'd been kidnapped as a child and they'd been looking for her since. "This makes no sense whatsoever. Why kidnap a child only to give it up?"

"I have a guess, but it's only that, a guess. What if whoever took her decided that it was too much work for them to have a child, and instead of going to jail for the kidnapping in the first place, they dumped her there?" Zak nodded, but that just didn't ring true either. He wondered if his parents had anything to do with this, but knew that they'd been dead long before Lindsey had been born. Even before her great-grandparents had been born. "Oh, and there's a grandmother too. She's pretty up there now, but she's been looking for her as well. There is a hefty reward out for her return. No questions asked."

"I have plenty enough for all of us." Zak had been sitting in the attorney's office, going over some of the paperwork that he'd been able to find on Lindsey, when Jed had called to him to tell him that not only was Lindsey talking, but she was telling him about the magic she now had. He was given a file, which still lay on his desk. Getting up and dressing himself quietly, he moved out of the room and to the dining room, a place where most of them worked on one project or another.

He wasn't surprised when, about an hour later, Lindsey came down to join him. She sat across from him after giving him a cup of tea, and then shared her plate of cookies with him. He was trying to decide how to start the conversation about her parents when she started talking about them. He sat up straighter in his chair and listened to her while she asked him about them.

"They're not dead, are they?" He shook his head. "I don't know how I know that, but when you came in the room tonight, I had a feeling that was what you were going to tell me."

"We'll have to run some tests to be sure. They still don't know yet, and until we confirm it, I think we should just keep it that way." She nodded, playing with her crumbs on the plate. "Lindsey, we never have to contact them if you don't want to."

"Yes, I do. I can't…they need to know that I'm here. And that I'm not…for a long time I thought of them coming for me. I knew that it was a dream of most kids in the place with me, but I really did have a lot of hope. Then as the months turned into years and then that seemed to stretch out too, I knew that they had no need of me. I had such high hopes that they'd have a change of heart and come back for me."

"How old were you when you were taken in at the home?" She told him she had no idea, but she'd been about eight, she thought. "The records that we've been able to find say that you were there longer than anyone. But there is no date of your being brought to them. He's digging deeper, but it looks like, other than your name listed as Lindsey Decker, there is nothing else."

"You mean my name might not even be Decker." He told her that as far as they could see it wasn't. "Do you know what it is then? I mean, you know who my parents might be. So what is my name?"

"Gabriella Cartwright. But that might not be it either. But you…." He got up and went to get the other file he'd been given. This one had a picture of her supposed family, including her parents as well as her grandmother. "You look like your mother, but it's the grandmother that you favor most."

Zak watched her as she looked at each picture. There were notes on the back of each one…the year that they'd been taken, and the name of the people who were in the photograph. The one of her grandmother looked to be about forty years old, with the woman standing beside a younger man. Zak knew it was the one that she held now.

"I met her only a few times. My grandmother, I think. She wasn't really thrilled about me. I don't remember the why of it now, but I remember her turning her nose up at me." Lindsey handed him the picture as she got up to refill the plate of cookies. And when she brought in a third cup and a pot this time, he smiled and shook his head when Jed joined them too. As he caught him up on what they'd been talking about, Lindsey looked at all the pictures again. She handed him one of the pictures that seemed out of place with the rest of them.

"Who is this man? I mean, I've seen him, but…I think he's the man that came to see me at the home a couple of times. And he made sure that I was always given more than the rest. Whatever that meant. There was never enough anyway." Zak took the picture and noticed that the name on the back was blurred, like it had been handled with damp fingers. "I think his name is Dean Landon. I mean, it might not be, but that's the name that sticks out in my head."

"I'll have someone look into it. Maybe he worked for the home you were at and was making sure things were right." He no more believed that than she appeared to. "Lindsey, this doesn't change how I feel about you. Not one bit."

"I know that, silly." She stood up and stretched, and Zak felt his cock fill. When she looked at him with a smile, he wanted to take her right there on the table. "Wanna take a long shower with me?"

He nearly fell getting up to go with her. And as soon as he got to the bedroom, it was all he could do not to simply take her against the wall. Would he ever get enough of her? He hoped not. Zak was in love with her.

Chapter 9

"And then what?" Asher looked around the big table, waiting on someone to answer his question. He didn't like this idea, and less so since there were no clear answers about it. "For all we know it could be the demon himself asking us to all be there when he's brought up from the earth, and then he'll kill us all."

"I don't think so." He wanted to glare at Lindsey, but she was a little on the scary side today. Twice now he'd heard the large dragon in the yard huff at the ground, and he didn't want to be hurt when he came in the house for him. "Look, I'll tell you what she looked like and you tell me if it was her or not."

"Won't work. None of us have seen her." Everyone looked at Simeon when he spoke. "I'm guessing Dad and Elbert have, but none of us have…you know what? I think Asher might be onto something here. I hate to admit it, but this just doesn't sound right."

"Why?" Asher flushed when they all turned to him. "I mean, why are you thinking I'm right all of a sudden?"

"If it is a demon, and I'm not saying that it is or not, then what's to say that he doesn't want us fucking with his lair? What better way to make us stop then to have us all lined up around a deep hole in the middle of the night? I mean, how many times did she tell you that we all had to be there? Did she give you a reason why we had to be?" Lindsey said that she hadn't. But Asher wasn't any more comfortable with this line of thought from Simeon than he'd been with going out there in the first place. "Then there is the whole thing about all twelve of us. Twelve men, she said. Twelve is not how many we are now, not with all of us. We're sixteen with Dad, Grandpa, you, and Essie. And I'm betting right now that Essie won't stay behind just because she was told to."

"You're right about that." Essie handed Asher a large plate of cookies, and he started to set them in front of him when she smacked him and told him to share. "I swear, Asher, you're like a small kid when it comes to sweets. But back to the demon. I've called the earth and there is something down there, as Lindsey has said, but they're not so sure that he's always been there."

"So, what do I do?" No one had an answer for Lindsey, and she huffed at them. "Look, this person came to me to do something for her. I'm not saying I want to do it either, but I'm thinking that if we don't do something, then whatever it is will do something more. Don't you think?"

"I do think you might be right on that." Grandda came in with a large platter of cookies, as well as some kind of pastry that Asher reached for. When he had his hand smacked, he looked at his grandda as he continued. "We are having a guest, and it would reflect badly on this household should I have to explain to her that you ate her favorite sweet."

"Caroline is coming?"

Asher sat up straighter in his chair. He wasn't afraid of her, not really. But she had a way about her that made him want to never piss her off. He looked around the table at the rest of them and noticed that they, too, were sitting a little straighter, as well as fixing their hair. She was a witch, after all.

"I am here." She sat down beside him and grinned at him. "You are no different now than when you were a small boy. Always trying to con someone out of their treats. Asher, your mother would have a fit to know that you still do that."

"I'm the oldest." Everyone laughed at him, and he felt his face heat up. He knew it was lame, but he'd been saying the same thing for centuries. Usually it never worked, but it didn't stop him from trying. "We're discussing this demon and the person who might have come to see Lindsey. Do you have any advice?"

"I do. I would do as was asked, but do it on your own terms. If it is the beast calling to her, then it will be simple enough to vanquish him. If it happens to be the queen, then she will think it funny that we have altered things a little to be sure." Caroline looked at Lindsey and smiled. "You are lovely, my dear. Can you let me touch your arm? I should like to know what you have been up to."

"I'm not sure that's a good idea." Caroline only nodded but didn't push Lindsey into doing anything she didn't want to. Asher also wasn't too sure it was the right idea right now. Too much information about someone was just that, too much. He much preferred getting to know someone the old fashion way. By conversation.

As the night wore on, it was decided that they'd go to the large opening during the day and see what they could find. But they were going to take Silco as well. His mate was close to birthing their young soon, and laying eggs was just as much work as a human birthing, or so he'd been told. So Silco was going but couldn't stay long. Asher thought it wonderful that he would be there during the first few hours.

As per custom, as king and queen, he and Essie would be there to bless the newborn. Lindsey would be as well. She told them that she, too, had a gift for the child, and that was when he'd thought of one as well. Grandda had told him that he was only to give the child a coin, one from the treasure house, and that would be enough. For some reason he'd thought there should be more, but Grandda had said it would be enough.

Asher moved into the yard after the rest went up to bed. Caroline was staying again, which he liked. Having her so close usually meant that things were going to go well. And he would really like for this to go well. When Jed joined him a little later, he sat on the porch and watched the stars dance across the sky.

"I'm supposed to tell you that Lindsey's parents are found." Asher knew this already, but was concerned by the tone that Jed had in telling him. "As you might have guessed, she's scared to meet them, and we know her grandmother."

"We do?" Jed nodded and told him her name. "That's her grandmother? Holy shit, how did she have such a wonderful granddaughter? That old biddy is not one I'd care to be working with, much less be related to. She is not a nice person."

"Yeah, I know. I never told her, of course, but I'd really like it if you and Essie were around when things get together. I guess the tests aren't back yet that we had done, so it might be for nothing." Asher nodded, knowing that she was going to be related to the bitch. "Her parents don't know that she's been found either. I don't know why, but I have a feeling that things are not going to be all teary and exciting. Just a feeling."

"You think that something else is going on?" Jed nodded, but said he didn't know what it might be. "Your instinct is usually right on. If you think things are going to be bad, then I'm with you. What do you think about this demon thing with Lindsey? I meant to ask you earlier but got sidetracked."

"Now that Caroline is here, I have no idea why, but I feel much better about it. And the fact that none of us are willing to just think this is right. Zak is under the impression that this demon knows what's in our heads and that is why he's able to play us. I hope you don't mind, but I had Caroline tighten the magic around here. That way he has no idea what our plan is." Asher told him it was a good idea. "I've also wanted to talk to you about building us a home. Not that I don't love living here, but I think that we need our own space. Especially since Lindsey wants to have a baby."

Asher had known this day was coming. They were already starting to get cramped up in the house with them there. And if the others had mates coming soon, it would be even worse. But he wanted his family here, close, where they'd always been. He looked out over the field where the big dragon had been lying until tonight.

"You know what I feel about us being together. We're better as a family than separated." Jed told him he agreed. "I know that it's going to be necessary for us to be on our own, and I think you're right about how much harder it would be once children start to come. I don't have to like it, but I know that it's going to happen."

"We don't want to move to another place. Here on the land would be perfect if you don't mind." Asher reminded him it was his land as well. "I know that, but you're in charge of us. And as much as you'd like to deny it, you always have been. I like knowing that you're in charge, if it matters to you."

"It does. Thank you." He tried to think how to tell him that it would hurt him to have him move out when Jed spoke again.

"I think that we'd like to build right across from here. There in the open field where we used to play as children." Asher looked out over the darkened field and thought of the trees they'd climbed, as well as the trouble they'd gotten into with their dad. "There's a nice plot behind where I'd like to build where Lindsey could garden. She's been helping Essie with her herbs and has mentioned that she'd like to grow some things as well. I think it would do her a world of good."

"She's doing well then?" Jed grinned and nodded. "Yeah, I thought so too. You guys look good together. And she seems to be fitting in well with all of us. This family thing, it will be over soon and it will be just a memory that we can sweep off the steps, as Mom used to say."

"Yeah. Oh, before I forget to tell you, there are some inspectors going out to the Cox place over the next few days. They got an anonymous tip saying there was a smell coming from the house. Not that they're going to find anything in the house but the boxes, but it was a good call to make." Asher asked him who they had called. "The postmaster. She was more than willing to do something about him. She said that he gives her workers a hard time when his mother's check is late, like it's their fault."

They'd already been to the house. Jed, his dad, and him had walked over there just this morning. And the boxes that Lindsey had told them about were just sitting there, all lined up. There were other things in the house as well, mementoes of the women that had their dad a little creeped out. The one that had him shiver was the lock of hair of the woman who had been killed first. It was hanging over the kitchen window like a flower in a vase, her name written on it in a crude hand.

"When they go out there, do they know that we don't know a thing?" Jed nodded and told him that he had already warned their attorney of the fact. "I guess having him served was a good thing too. I hate to toss anyone out on their asses, but this guy was not going to get away with killing anyone."

"He won't. And I let Lindsey know too. In the event that someone comes around while she's here alone. I don't want to shield her overly much, but this thing with Cox rattled her pretty good." It had rattled them all. The big dragon Silco had saved them all, he was sure of it. "There's one more thing I need to talk to you about. I want to go into business with Zak and open a place in town. I have a hankering to open an antique shop. We have enough stuff in storage that we can unload and make a little on the side too. I'm thinking of donating most of the money to a homeless shelter in town. People like Lindsey could have used something like that at one time or another."

"We have so much in storage, I bet you could open two shops and never run out of inventory." Jed laughed with him. "Go for it. I might have a few of the locals come in and see if they want to buy some of it too. There is this large armoire that Kenny, the guy who runs the hardware store, has been bugging me about for years."

After deciding on a name, Castle Antiques, they headed into the house. Asher decided that with his power and magic he could have the house built for his brother in a few hours, and started on it. He knew that any changes that Jed would want would be easy to fix, but for the most part, the house would be complete by morning. He was smiling when he entered their bedroom. He stood in the doorway watching the couple on the bed.

Kiaran was eating Essie, and she was sobbing out her releases. When they spied him standing there, he nearly fell onto her when she begged him to come and let her suck his cock. As soon as he was inside of her mouth and fucking her, Kiaran went back to what he was doing.

Christ, this was the best. Having a woman between them was more than he could ever have hoped for. His cock ached to fill her pussy, but watching Kiaran enjoy her too made him fuck her all the harder. And when he came, filling her with his cum, he heard her scream again as Kiaran went back on his heels and fisted his own release over the two of them. Asher knew he was going to be getting little sleep again tonight. And was thrilled about it.

~~~

The house was beautiful. As Lindsey walked around it, all she could think about was that it belonged to her, and the men in her life, but it was her very first home. Even the bedrooms, all four of them, were lovely, with the wallpaper looking old fashioned and the four poster beds perfectly matched to each room. She ran her hand over the oak dresser that was in their room, and turned to look at Jed when he cleared his throat.
~~~

"Asher said that he could change each room to how we wanted it. I think you like it just the way it is, but I might be wrong." Tears filled her eyes at how happy she was, and he came toward her. "Don't cry, honey. If you don't like it, we can build on our own. He just thought he was being helpful."

"I love everything about it and don't want a thing changed. And the kitchen. Did you see it? I could get lost in how big it is." He held her, and she smiled at the way the pantry had been filled to nearly overflowing. "Now all I have to do is learn how to use most of that stuff. I have no idea what a couple of those things are."

"Zak loves to cook, and I'm sure he knows what they are." Jed kissed her head. "As for the rest of the house, we'll need to get things too to fill it out. He can only work with a few things with his magic, and to be honest with you, I had no idea he could make a fridge and stove. But I think that Essie's magic helps there as well."

"I met her dad this morning. He's very strange, isn't he?" Jed stiffened in her arms, and she looked up at him. "What is it?"

"You met Abraham? When?" She stepped back from the anger in his voice. "I'm not mad at you, love, but Abraham isn't near here. He left here several months ago to stay with Caroline. She is helping him acclimate himself to this century."

"He was in the field near the big cave. I didn't go to him, but he sort of appeared there. I didn't care for him, if you want to know the truth of it. He was rude and very…he asked a lot of questions that I never answered." Lindsey tried to think what he'd looked like and came up blank. "I don't know what he looks like to describe him to you. I'm betting that…it's because I didn't know the real one, so he had to fake it, didn't he?"

"Yes. He more than likely wanted to get you alone and that's why he met you there. Did he mention the pit? Or the demon?" She said that he had, several times. "He's trying to figure out if we're going to do as he asked. All of us get together like Zak's mother had suggested."

"So it was never the queen that came to see me, just as Asher said." Jed nodded and told her that it was a good thing to know. "I know, but it was sort of cool to think that she'd reached out to me. And this demon, what do we do about him now? I'm assuming that I can't call him out and get rid of him."

"No, but I know someone that can. Caroline has been hiding in the house since she got here. I'm betting that he has no idea that she's around. Because if he did, I'm sure that he'd not have approached you like he did." Lindsey looked around the room again and marveled at how quickly things had soured. "He won't be able to come to the house. There is a great deal of magic here, and that is keeping us all safe. But for the time being, stay around the houses. I'm not sure that he'd not resort to something to get to us."

She told him that she would and went back to the kitchen with him. There were things in the pantry to eat, but there were no staples. Milk and butter for one thing, and eggs. Lindsey thought about raising chickens here, but decided that they might not care for the idea. But the longer it simmered in her head, the more appealing it became. She mentioned it to Jed in a passing sort of way.

"Chickens for eggs? I love the idea. And it would make it so that Grandda didn't have to go into town every few days for them. What about a barn and a couple of milking cows? We could even learn to care for them as well." She was warming to the idea, and even to the garden that he told her that he'd asked Asher for. "You might want to start smaller than he put in, but I think it'll be fun for us all to have fresh things. I know that while Zak and the others don't eat a lot of green things, they will eat them. But I enjoy a nice salad once in a while."

It was cold now and getting colder, but spring wasn't as far off as it looked. In a few short months she could plow up her garden and get it ready for things like tomatoes and corn. Giddy with it now, she asked if she could use his computer to look at seed catalogs.

"We need to get you a computer of your own. And I think Zak and I are going to open a business. I know you said you were good at filing and all, but what if you helped us out with our books? It might be fun for us all to work together." Lindsey told him she loved the idea. "Good. We already looked at a building, and we think we might be open as soon as the New Year. Asher said that we have enough to keep us filled up; antiques, I mean."

As they talked, like a real couple, Zak joined them. They decided to grill out and realized that they had nothing to use. Laughing about how they had a great deal but very little to actually go with things, they built a fire with Zak's help and cooked the steaks out on the open flame. As she baked some potatoes, Lindsey realized how much she loved being here. And with these two. They were her life, and as far as she was concerned, everyone and everything else could just leave them alone.

As they enjoyed their dinner, Jed told her stories of them growing up in the area. How it had been to be with dragons and five brothers. Zak told about the Christmases they'd had as a family, and how Sally, their other mother, had never made them feel any less a part of the household than blood.

"She'd knit us the most amazing scarfs and sweaters. One year I got one from her that had this huge dragon on the back of it. I think I wore it well into summer, never wanting to take it off because she'd made it just for me. I fully expected her to make them all one the following year, but she didn't. It was the only one I think she ever made." Zak smiled softly at the memory, and Lindsey felt her heart overflow with love.

"I go to her grave and talk to her sometimes. I see that she…there is so much love in her headstone. I know that she can't hear me, but I just tell her about what I've been up to and what I'm doing. I even told her that I love you guys." Lindsey picked up their plates and took them to the kitchen, glad that no one followed her. Standing looking out the window, she saw a small bird and realized it might have been injured. Going out onto the porch, she realized two things at once.

It wasn't a bird, and it was hurt.

The dragon, small and scared, moved to stand in front of her before she could call to the others. Essie came out of their house and moved toward her until Lindsey put up her hand to stop her. The dragon might be small, but Lindsey had a feeling that it was a great deal more powerful than it looked for its size.

"I felt it. Only when it touched the ground. Do you know what's wrong with her?" Lindsey felt Jed and Zak come out onto the porch, but they didn't move toward her as Essie continued. "Asher is getting Elbert. I think he's in the back field."

"I'm not going to harm you." The dragon, about four or five inches tall and with her tail about twelve inches long, sat down on her hind feet and stared at her. "Can you tell me your name?"

"Daisy." Lindsey nearly laughed at the odd name, but only nodded. "They told us that you'd be able to speak to us. I didn't want to believe them. It's been so long since…where are the king and queen?"

When she pointed to Essie and now Asher, Daisy made her way to them. She moved slowly, and that was when she noticed the mark on her back. Someone had hurt her recently. Lindsey asked her about it.

"There is one that would have us for his trophy room. I have only just gotten away with my life." She turned to look at Lindsey as she stopped moving to Asher and Essie. "You can help me? I should like to be healed should he come here to get me and the others."

"How many more of you are there, do you know?" Daisy said that she'd been with two others when they'd crested the mountain, but the man had been waiting for them. Lindsey told them what the dragon had said.

"He killed one of us. The other, I don't know. He was flying higher than myself and Darthmeth were, but he disappeared as soon as we saw the man. I think Salomon was pulling his attention away from us."

Zak said he'd go and look for him and shifted to his dragon. As soon as he was gone, Daisy bowed to the king and queen of dragons and then stared openly at Caroline. It was then that Lindsey realized how old all these people were. Caroline had been around so long that she had more than likely met all the dragons that were coming to them.

An hour after Daisy had found a place to rest, Zak returned. He had the body of the other female in his claws and the male was holding onto his back. Darthmeth had been killed by magic, it was determined…the same magic that had injured Salomon. He would live, but it would be a while before he'd be able to fly. Elbert was caring for him when Zak took the small body of Darthmeth to the field to give her a proper dragon burial.

"What is that? A proper dragon burial?" Elbert nodded to a book on the dresser, and Lindsey picked it up. "This is beautiful."

"It was my own king and queen's. They had it for generations, and when I was to help Sally and Jacob, they read it as well. Caring for dragons is not easy. You may use it, if you wish." She told him that she would. "It is magical. If you need something, put your hand over the dragons then ask it, in dragon speak, and it will take you to the page. Or you may read it from cover to cover. I would suggest that you do the latter for the fact that you'll understand more than most."

"Because I can talk to them." He told her that was some of it. "And what else? Do you know something, I don't…well, I know you do, but I mean about myself and this book?"

"You are mentioned in the pages. Your name is there with the others to come. Do not show them what you find, but since you are able to speak the language, you can read it as well." She nodded and told him that neither Zak nor Jed could read it, and she'd thought that strange. "'Tis not strange, but the way things are. Read it. I shall be happy for the chance to share the knowledge."

Lindsey had a feeling that she'd be a good deal more confused than helpful, but said nothing as they tended to Salomon's wounds.

Chapter 10

Everyone stood around the open area. Jacob was scared, if truth be known, but he knew that if they were going to get this done, then that thing had to be taken care of. He had a feeling that the monster had played a part in the deaths of the king and queen, but hadn't said anything to anyone but his Sally. She had, of course, agreed with him.

You keep our boys safe, now you hear me? He told her that he'd rather die again than to let them be hurt. *And you don't be getting yourself all tangled up either. I'm not there to tend to you now, and you might not get the proper healing.*

"I got me Elbert. That man can heal about anything." She told him that she knew that. "Lindsey's got herself a right fine job. Did I tell you that she can speak with dragons?"

You did. What you failed to mention is that there are two more on the land. I knew little Daisy when she was just a hatchling. You should remember her too. Her parents had named her that hoping for the good graces of the earth to keep her safe, remember? He did now that she reminded him. *Born in the dead of winter. Snow up to our bottoms, and they're naming a dragon Daisy. Poor thing was made fun of for decades.*

"That she was, that she was." He laughed as he pulled weeds around her stone. "I got me some plants coming in. Lindsey and Essie are gonna help me plant them for you. Myrtle of all things. You can just go out and pull it up like a weed, and they're ordering it from some computer thing."

It will be tamer, Lindsey told me. He'd been told the same thing, but he liked the wildness of it. *What are you going to do about the man that hunts them? If he finds them all on the land, he'll make trouble for you all. I wish I was there to help.*

"Me too, my love. I miss you more and more every day." He lay back against the post that had been there since the day he'd put his only true love in the ground. "Jed and the others have them a house now. Asher put it up for them, but I think that little Lindsey would have been thrilled with a tent if they gave it to her. She's all excited to be having a meal. Had to send them boys off to get her some proper things to cook with. And I got her a grill. Not one of them fancy kinds that you can put cold stuff in, but a regular one. Mayhap she'll have me over for a meal or two soon."

She loves you. Talks about you all the time when she comes to see me. He had to think if he'd done anything to warrant him getting into trouble with his wife when she laughed at him. *You old goat. You know that she'd never tell me a thing that you'd done wrong. But don't you think for a minute that I don't know.* He nodded, then remembered she couldn't see him.

"Tomorrow we're gonna confront us that demon. I'm not sure what we're going to do with him, but we're going to do it. Lindsey said we'd do it our way and not his, in any case." He thought of how passionate she'd been about it and smiled. "Got her a fine temper, she does. But I like her idea."

Jed touched his arm and it took him from his memories of his wife. He had to blink several times to realize that he'd missed something, and when Jed smiled, Jacob told him he was sorry. Thinking about his wife would take away the worse kind of thoughts for him.

"Are you ready, Dad?" Jacob nodded and moved to stand where he'd been told…out of sight. Not because they didn't think he could help, but they were going to show the man, or whatever he was, who was in charge. And this demon wasn't. "Just come out when we call for you. All right?"

"Sure, sure, I got it. Don't want him thinking he's in charge." It was full sunlight, and the moon, when it came up, was only a quarter. A full moon wasn't for a few more weeks. Also, there were only going to be six of them, not all that he'd made sure of. And they were protected in a way that would not allow them to get hurt. Even Jacob had some of it spread all over him. Magic to keep them all safe and sound.

He could see everything from the place he was standing. Lindsey was standing with Caroline, and Essie, Asher, and Kiaran were with Jed and Zak. They were impressive looking, Jacob thought. He'd think twice about messing with them, should it come to that. When Caroline cleared her throat, he moved just out of sight should the demon come out.

"Show yourself." Jacob nearly laughed. Nothing about Caroline was showy. If she wanted you to do something, by using her magic, you'd bet your bottom dollar you'd be doing it. And she never wasted words either. Come out or just do it was more her style.

The ground rumbled a little, but he didn't take his eyes off what was going on. The rest of them, all his boys and even Elbert in his great dog, were close, too, should they need them. While little Salomon was still laid up, Daisy had even gone deep into the pit just this morning to tell them what she'd seen, which wasn't much. And Silco, a proud new daddy, was on the hillside and could be at their side in moments. Everything was set.

There was a blur of movement at first. Then, as the creature pulled himself to just the top of the rim of the hole, it was clear that he was much bigger than they'd thought. But he wasn't going to be any kind of trouble for these people. Or so Jacob hoped.

"You are not who I called to come here. Where are the rest?" The creature, a dark and smelly being, looked at Lindsey. "You were to bring them all to me. I cannot have you here now. The sun burns my skin. Come later, on the night of a full moon, and we will talk again."

As he started to move down into the hole again, Caroline lifted her hands, as did Essie. He knew what they were about, but it was still a surprise to watch. The ground pushed the creature out of the hole, and he sat on the cold earth like he was a prized turkey at a shoot.

"You have no rights to do this. Unhand me." The creature looked around as if to see who else was there. "You cannot do this to me. I demand that you put me back."

"The home you have lived in is now sealed against you." He roared at Caroline when she told him what was going on. "And now you will be tried against the harm that you caused this earth."

"You should have done as I asked." The thing sat up, his body taking the shape of a man but much larger than any that he'd ever seen. "I have lived here for many, many years, and I shall continue to do so. The king has given me permission. If he were here, he'd tell you that he had."

"I am king." The creature stopped in mid-shift, his body still partly human but mostly creature, a blob of a thing that was smelling worse and worse as he baked in the sunlight. "And even if you were given such permission, I'm revoking it as of now. You have lived here long past the time that was given to you."

"Lies." But even Jacob could see that the thing was afraid. "You lie to me. I have permission to live as I please. There is no one to gainsay me. Not even you."

"I have spoken. And what I say is law."

Jacob was proud of the tone his son had, the way that he seemed to grow with each word. But then he was shoved back, and it was all Jacob could do not to run to his side. The only thing that kept him in place was his darling wife telling him to stay put.

Lindsey moved forward, her hand outstretched as she moved toward the creature. As soon as she touched him, her fingers only just touching his flesh, the creature cried out, his skin blistered where her fingers had been. When she took her hand away, he could see that she, too, had been hurt, but nothing like the thing had.

"Your name is Slug. And you were warned, long ago, that you were not only not welcome in the castle keep, but that to return would mean certain death. You defied the king even then." The creature was still screaming, his body contorting into several shapes at once. But his true self, the slug, was coming out more and more. "Helena, the Black Witch, brought you here when she was employed. In that, you were to give her any information you could that would help her cause. The one where she was to kill the king and queen."

"I gave her it all, too. It was not my fault that the hatchlings were never known to me. I would have killed them myself should I have known where they were." Slug glared at Lindsey when she laughed at him. "You will die, creature of the earth. And when you are dead, I will feast upon your body as I have done all the ones in this keep. I will eat away at your body and grow even bigger because of it."

"I don't think so. Even as we stand here talking to you, your flesh is melting off you. Your slimy skin is falling to the ground like the unwanted nastiness that you are." He watched as Lindsey laughed again, her head thrown back with it, and Jacob couldn't help but smile. She was as fearless as any of her sons were. "What do you suppose will come of you should you try to crawl your way back into that hole? I know, do you?"

"You will die." She told him that he'd said that before. As soon as he moved toward them, Jacob felt the dragon on the hill. It wasn't him that he felt so much as his great wings shifting the foundation of the earth. Trees bent to his will as he moved to land beside Asher and the others. "What is the meaning of this? You cannot have them here. The dragons are all dead. I saw them dead. Their hatchlings broken open and empty from their shell."

"I think you should have another look, Slug. The king's children are here. Their strength as great as their sire's, and their mother's magic running through them like a river down a hill." Caroline nodded to the rest of them, and one by one, the sons of the king came to shift in front of him. "See them? See what great offspring that they had even though you murdered them in their home? The children of Anthony and Eve live on. And more generations of them will come to pass. You have failed, Slug. And the witch Helena is dead as well."

He moved back from Silco as he stood up on his hind legs. He was enormous in his glory, his golden wings spread out wide so as to protect the others from his flame. Even as Jacob moved to the place he'd been told to go should Silco help them, all he could think about was that he wished his mate were here now. That his lovely Sally could see what their children, all of them, had done to protect the area and them in turn.

The screams would haunt him for a time, he knew this. The creature did not die quickly, nor quietly either. He was gone by the time Jacob was told he could come out of the rock formation that he'd been in, and when he looked at the earth, scorched now as the earth had been when the other monster had been killed, all he could think about was his Sally and how hurt she'd be from this stain. He moved to stand near the smoldering tree and put his hand near it, feeling its pain as Sally had taught him to do.

"I can help it." He looked at Caroline when she came to stand beside him. "It's why we put him here and not in the clearing. There is very little dirt beneath his spot, mostly stone that can take the heat better. The tree, he said that he would gladly take the heat if it meant that others could live in his area."

Jacob looked around and realized that there was very little in this area. He'd thought it was because of the castle, but he could see now that the deadness of the area stretched beyond the area to include some of the trees too. He now wondered how much the slug had harmed this earth in his pursuit of living where he was not welcome.

Essie and Caroline worked on the ground. They'd called in their friend Gobi, the witch who lived in town and ran the little shop. Even her trailer, the one that she took to shows for extra income, was filled with all sorts of pots, most of them filled with trees and other plants that he'd not seen in a long while. He and the boys began planting them where they were told.

He saw Lindsey talking to the stone that was his wife's, and said he needed a small break.

"I don't know what to do with them." He wondered what she was talking about when she turned and laid a bunch of little pots along the front of Sally's headstone. "I have to go and look them all up there are so many, but I wanted to bring these out to you. I know from Zak that you loved roses, but I think you'll enjoy these as well."

When she pulled a small spade from her pocket, he started to go and help her. But Sally asked him to wait, that she wanted to have her near for a while. As Lindsey began turning over the soil, she also continued talking as if Sally were there.

"My parents are going to be here soon. The DNA test that I told you about confirmed that they're my biological parents. I wish you were here. The others, the boys as Jacob calls them, said you'd know just what to say to them." Jacob thought perhaps Lindsey would as well, but stayed back. "That's not the only reason I wish you were here. I'm not…I love Essie very much, but I've never had a mother before. Not one that I wanted to be with. I think we'd get along just fine."

The pot of something moved on the ground, and it took Jacob only a second to know that his Sally had done that. Lindsey sat back on her heels and watched the little pot move, not saying a word.

"Can you hear me?" The little pot seemed to rattle back and forth as if it were saying yes. "And can you see me?" This time the pot moved in a circle, saying no instead of yes.

She sat there for a few minutes. Jacob could well imagine what she was thinking. Was she nuts or was a dead woman talking to her? He sat down on the ground to watch the two of them, enjoying this more than he could say.

~~~

Lindsey wasn't sure whether her fuzzy mind was playing tricks on her or not, but she sat down and picked up the little plastic pot before putting it back. She was nuts, she decided, when she realized that she wanted to talk to this woman.

"I'm not sure what to tell you. I'm guessing you know who I am and what I'm doing here." The pot nodded at her. "This is sort of creepy. Do I have to bring a pot each time I come to see you now so we can talk?"

The little flowers that she'd planted moved this time. It was yarrow, Gobi had told her, and it would bloom to be a yellow so bright that it would blot out the sun. Now its stems were shaking in a perfect head-shaking motion.

"I see. So you can use whatever is here to answer me. I'm assuming it must be yes or no questions." The plant nodded at her. "Okay. That could be hard, but not something we can't work around."

Lindsey looked beyond the small cemetery and then back at the headstone. "We have our home now. I've never had one before. I've been in apartments, of course. Do you know what those are?" The plant said that it did. "I guess even if you've been gone for a while, you would
~~~

be able to keep up with things. Your sons, they come to talk to you as well, don't they?"

When she had her answer, Lindsey leaned back against the post that held up the fence surrounding them. "I want to be a good wife to them both, you know? Keep them happy and safe. I also want a baby. Well, lots of them. But I don't know…do you know if I'm going to be buried here when I pass?"

She watched the little plant as it moved. It was shaking its head at her, and she felt hurt that she'd not be buried in such a pretty place. When the voice drifted over her, it was soft and feminine, and Lindsey knew it was Mrs. Sally. "Forever," it told her. Lindsey sat there thinking of what that word might mean for her.

"You're telling me I'm not going to die?" This time it told her no. "I'm not going to die, or you're telling me that I'm wrong?"

"Forever," the voice told her again. Then it said, "You, forever."

She was going to live forever. While this was good news, she supposed, she had all kinds of questions. Like living forever. What did it mean? She supposed that she'd be like Jed and the rest of them, sort of immortal. But would she get sick? Did she have to…she didn't know, be careful of certain things? As she sat there contemplating what she'd just learned, Jacob came to sit beside her.

"You're going to think I'm insane, but I think I just talked to your long dead wife." He nodded. "You talk to her too."

"I do." He picked up the small pot that had been the beginning of her insanity. "She wishes you'd not think of yourself as insane. She said that you are as sane as she is."

"You really do talk to her. And she was talking to me through these plants." Jacob nodded and told her that his wife had been a white witch. "So, that's why she can move them…and Essie, did she get her power from her too?"

"No. Essie is a faerie. One of the strongest we know of. And in all the years we've been around, there have been a great many of them coming and going." He sat the little pot back on the dirt. "Sally wants you to finish telling her about your parents. She would like to know what you plan to do about them."

"About them? I have no idea. I don't want them to come here. I know that much." And she didn't either, although she'd only just realized that. "I love it here. And Jed and Zak…I have no idea why I think so, but these people will intrude on this, and I don't want to share it with them. They might be the nicest people in the world. But they were never there for me, and right now I've decided that I don't need them."

"Sally said good for you." Jacob sat up a little and began brushing the small leaves that had blown up on the grave and headstone since she'd been out there. "My Sally was the greatest woman I knew, or have since. You and Essie are good girls and I love you like my own, but my Sally, she would have made you feel very welcome. It was her way."

"You have made me feel welcome and a part of your family." He only nodded at her. "You miss her very much, don't you?"

"I do. The biggest part of my heart lays here. I don't think…if I had known how it would feel to be here without her, I'm not sure that I would have made myself known to them boys. I miss her something terrible." Lindsey put her hand over his, and he looked at her. "You remind me of her a bit. Essie, too, but in a different way. And when you stood up to that monster today, nearly burst my heart with pride for you. Sally would have just loved to have been there too, she told me."

"I love you, Jacob. More than...I've never had a dad before that I can remember. And the one that's coming in a few days to see me, he might be nice too. But you are the only man, other than Jed and Zak, that I will ever love like this." He took her hand to his mouth and kissed it noisily. "You did a great job, you and Mrs. Sally, in raising these men up to be kind and good. I don't know what I would have done had they not saved me."

"You would have done all right on your own. You already went and got away from that man, and over the next few weeks, they'll find them other girls and give them some peace as well." She nodded at him and helped him clean the debris off the grass. "You might think it's silly, me doing this, but I can't think of dirt being on her face and body. She was just perfect, and I want to keep her that way even now."

Lindsey glanced over at the other headstone, the one that marked Jacob's passing. The blanket had blown off earlier and she'd put it back, but he'd been loved as well, just as much as his wife. She wondered if he knew that. Or had his children ever told him how much they loved him? Lindsey knew that for as long as she lived—and according to Mrs. Sally that was going to be a good long time—she would tell the men in her life how much she loved them. And Essie too. Life was going to be surrounded by love from now on, even if she had to beat people into seeing it her way.

As they made their way back to the house, Jacob was telling her about seeing this house for the first time, and how much he'd been in awe of the number of rooms. He laughed as he told her how he'd never dreamed that he'd really have six sons, and that they'd be the hosts to such wonderful men too.

"That king was a good man. He was a might rushed when I spoke to him that night, but he made sure that everything was set to rights for us. And his boys too. Never wanted for a thing, we didn't. Elbert was the best thing that could have been there for us when they started coming. And my Sally, she taught every one of us how to read and write. I could even add up a set of numbers if I'm pressed to do it. Yes, ma'am, life then was nothing like it is now. Not one bit. But I loved it all the same."

Lindsey was still laughing when she entered the house, and knew right away that something had happened.

"Your family is here, all of them. They're here, in town. And they want to meet you." Lindsey sat down next to her men and thought about what Asher was telling her. "We won't let them hurt you. You're family now, and we're going to show them that if they try any shit with you. You see if we don't."

She wasn't worried so much about them hurting her as trying to take her away from all this. And she was damned if they were going to get away with it. Letting out a long breath, she looked at Jed and Zak.

"You'll go with me?" They both nodded and told her that they all were going. "Good. I don't know why, but I'm worried that they'll try something, and I don't want to have to go to prison. I just found out that I'm an immortal, and I don't want to spend all that time behind a set of bars."

Chapter 11

Millicent was not used to having to wait on anyone. People waited on her, not the other way around. And this office was beneath her. No one here seemed to realize that she was not their usual client. When the door beyond her opened, she huffed at her son and his wife.

"You are late." Donald nodded at her, but Gabby—what a horrid name—only smiled. The last ten years had been both a blessing and a trial since she'd forbidden the woman to speak to her. And now that she wanted to hear her snipe and whine about how she'd been treated, she wouldn't open her mouth. It didn't stop Millicent from digging at her, however. "Wherever did you get that dress? Off the rack at some discount store? When we get back to the hotel, you will burn it. Or so help me, I will."

Millicent wouldn't do that, of course, but no one but her knew it. Gabby would do as she was told and even show her the ashes of her work if she asked her for them. The woman was just too easy now. Even after all these years as her daughter-in-law, Millicent, still hated the very ground that she walked on. And now this.

The granddaughter had been found. It wasn't something that she'd ever thought would happen, and worse yet, by the time that she'd found out about her, the tests were already confirmed and there was no doubt as to who she was. Millicent was going to get to the bottom of this and heads were going to roll when she found out who had neglected to tell her about it. She knew that Donald was happy. But she was not.

The woman who had shown them into this shabby excuse for a waiting room came in a few minutes later. She asked them if they wanted anything to drink, and before she could tell the bitch to go away, Gabby ordered a glass of wine. It was barely five in the afternoon and she was drinking already. When the woman disappeared, Millicent turned to Gabby.

"Drunk again, are you?" Actually, she'd never seen either of them intoxicated since the disappearance of their child, and that rankled her too. There was little to nothing that she could hold over their heads anymore. When neither of them answered her, she decided to get as much information as she could about what the hell they were doing. "Where is it you're taking me? I know that they think they found your child, but where did they dig this one up?"

"Ohio." Her son. He'd been nasty to her for the last several years, and when she asked him what was going on, all he had said was, she should know. When nothing more was forthcoming, she turned and looked out the window. This had to stop.

Her money was gone. Every penny that she needed to live was given to her by Donald. And when she ran out, which was quite often, he would tell her to learn to spend better. Not him, of course, but his attorney. And that was happening more and more often lately. They only communicated through his lawyer.

To be honest with herself—and she seldom was with her or other people—she'd never had money. She'd appeared to have it, and that had suited her just fine until she'd been caught without the funds to cover her ass and her son had to bail her out. But he'd not done it graciously or without demands. The one that really made her tow the line was that she was never to come to their home on any occasion, nor was she to talk to the press. If she did, then everything would be gone.

Her husband had been the same demanding, mean kind of man. He'd had a lot of money too, and had always rubbed it in her face that she'd been as poor as a church mouse, and would die that way as well. She supposed that having an affair right at the beginning of her marriage to him and getting caught had embittered him toward her. But what did he expect her to do with all her free time if he wasn't going to give her money?

The affairs had continued over the years. And when she'd gotten pregnant with Donald, her darling, loving husband had demanded a DNA test to make sure that the baby was his before he'd even pay the first bill. Then after it was proven that Donald was indeed his, he never touched her again, not even to hold her hand when they went to functions.

Millicent looked up when she heard them talking. Gabby was laughing at something that Donald had said, and he was glowing with it. Damned idiot. Didn't he see what she was? A money whore. And the worst part of it was, there wasn't a damned thing that Millicent could do about it. Not since the disappearance of that child.

"The attorney will see you now." The same woman from before had come in to get them. Millicent stood up to follow, still trying to reason why she was here too, when the woman looked at her. "I'm sorry, miss. This is for family only."

"I'm his mother." No one moved, and she was sure that Donald was going to leave her behind. He'd done this entire thing to humiliate her again. "Tell them, Donald. This is my grandchild too."

His short nod got her in, but she was seething when she was given a chair at the back of the room. Gabby sat up close to the desk, as did Donald, and she saw no reason why she should not be a part of this. It wasn't the child anyway. She'd made sure of that.

"Well, Mr. Cartwright, I'm calling you in today because we have a positive match on the DNA." Millicent stood up and everyone turned to her. "May I help you?"

"I don't...are you sure it's her? I mean, maybe she faked it. After all this time, it can't be her." Or it had better not be her. She'd gone to great lengths to make sure that the child was never heard from again. She wasn't going to inherit her parents' money, either. "I mean, things like this, mistakes on this sort of thing happen all the time, right?"

"There is no mistake. The woman known as Lindsey Decker is your daughter." Gabby started crying and Donald held her. The lawyer continued, but Millicent was still trying to work out what had gone wrong. She'd paid that man a great deal of money, money that she'd never had, to get rid of the brat.

"When can we see her?" That was a good question Gabby asked, as much as she hated to admit it. Where the hell had she been hiding all this time, and why the fuck didn't someone tell her? You'd think after twenty years someone would have said something.

Of course, had she waited a minute or two before killing the man who she had bargained with, she might have learned that he'd failed at killing the child. How hard could it have been to drop her off in the middle of a minority infested neighborhood and just leave her? Hell, she'd done it before and it wasn't that difficult.

"The family…I'm to understand that she's married to someone now. He and his family are due to arrive tonight." Donald asked him who they were. "Their name is…let me see. I have is somewhere."

As he searched his desk for the name, Millicent tried to think if the child would be able to remember her, or the man that had grabbed her from the house. She purposefully had drugged Donald and Gabby that night, and when the coast was clear, Landon had come in with his brother and they'd taken the drugged child and left with her. It was the last time she'd seen the brother or the girl. That might have just come back to bite her in the ass. When Millicent realized that the room was quiet, she looked around.

"Mother."

She nodded and stood up as well. She had no idea what was going on, but right now her ass was tighter than a knot in a balloon. Her mind was racing all the way back to the hotel. She knew that she was staying in the same one as her son and Gabby, but was not sure where they were in the big place. And when the limo stopped and she was handed out, it took her several moments to realize that she wasn't going to be going with them to meet the child. The limo that she'd been in disappeared as she stood there.

"Madam?"

She looked at the man dressed in a suit and tie. His name tag proclaimed him to be Theodore, but she really didn't care who he was. She was embarrassed. Wanting to ask him where they had gone and why she wasn't with them, she moved past him and stood at the door, waiting for him to open it for her. The lobby of the hotel wasn't grand, but it was clean and fresh. Going up to her room, she wondered what she should do now. First and foremost she had to find out where her granddaughter was and who the hell she was with.

How many Landons could there be in this area? She looked in vain for a phone book, and was told by the front desk that they no longer carried them. How the hell did you not have a phonebook? Instead of her asking that question and no doubt getting an equally ridiculous answer, Millicent hung up and started to pace the room.

This was going to end badly for her. She'd not had a great track record of late, and this was going to tip the scales so that her son would cut her off completely. He'd been threatening her for months now. Her spending was too much. She'd lied to people about what she was worth. She'd ordered herself a new fur, and he'd gone through the ceiling when the bill had been sent to him instead of the post office box that she had things like that sent to. Not that she collected the mail that often, but it had helped her in a pinch. Now the child was back.

Millicent had never liked the girl. She'd seen her only the few times, and that had been more than enough. And then there had been this big to-do over her sixth birthday and Millicent not being invited. Before that, she'd been working on a plan—not a good one, but a plan all the same—to have her son and his wife killed so that she'd get it all. Then there was the talk, the one that her son insisted on having in his office with his secretary there…as a witness, he'd called her. Donald had told her that he was writing his own mother out of his will. That everything would go to the child.

"You mean if anything happens to you and Gabby, I'll have the funds to raise her?" He'd shaken his head at her and told her no. "What do you mean, no? I'm her grandmother. I might not care to be called that, nor do I want all that much to do with the thing, but I am her grandmother, and if, God forbid, anything happens to the two of you, I can take her in and raise her in your home."

"No. If anything happens to us, then she will become a ward of Margo and Aldo. They'll take care of her and see that she gets all that she wants and needs. You'll not have anything to do with her." She asked him why she couldn't do that for him. "Because, as you said, you don't care for her, and I simply don't trust you to do what's right for her but only for yourself. You'd go through her money in no time, spending it on yourself, and Gabriella would be left with nothing."

She couldn't even deny it. It was not that she would have left the thing to starve. There were servants in his house, but to say it out loud and in front of that woman had been the final straw. It had taken her another year and a half to find someone to kidnap the brat, and then after all this time, she was showing up again.

Millicent wished now that she'd paid more attention to the attorney. Maybe she could have called them up and made them an offer to not show for this meeting. Or she could have gone to see the girl first and see if she knew who she was. It would be a longshot after all this time, but the way her luck was running, the girl would have said that she'd been there that night and so had the Landon men.

By the time she was dressed for dinner, she wasn't sure if she could go through with this. She'd packed and unpacked twice in the time that her son had been gone, and decided that she'd have to see what fell. There wasn't anywhere for her to go, but she counted on him not wanting to harm his mother. He might talk a lot, but Donald was her only son. And there was no way her only son would put her out in the cold.

Just as she was sitting down to her meal, a note was given to her. They'd been found, or at least the girl had been. Now she had to go and see to it that no one knew of her involvement in all this.

~~~

Lindsey was nervous. They'd all come with her to town, including Elbert and Jacob. As they sat in the upstairs banquet room that they'd reserved in the nice restaurant, all she could think about was she was doing just fine without her parents. Why on earth did they want to see her now?

"It'll be all right. You'll see." She nodded at Jed, who had not left her side since they'd entered. Zak was close, too, but he seemed to be keeping an eye on things for her. Keeping her safe. Calm and safe was what she needed to be right now.

"I've spoken to Donald, your father." Lindsey nodded at Asher as he took a seat. "If it makes you feel any better, he's more nervous than you are. And your mother, Gabby, hasn't stopped asking me if you were all right with this."

"They don't want to see me?" Asher told her that they really did. "I don't know why. I mean, I've been this close to them for all this time and no one found me. Why now?"
~~~

"Because they never stopped looking." Lindsey knew this. The attorney had told her the same thing a few days ago when he'd come to the house on another matter. "This will be fine. And if it's not, we all get to have a nice meal, then we go home. It's as simple as that."

She nodded again at Asher, knowing that nothing was ever simple. There were simpletons, but never simple things. Things never seemed to happen just the way you'd think they would, and rarely did she come out on top. When the door opened, she nearly squeaked when a woman came in, but it was only the waitress. She was bringing in pitchers of water for the tables. Squeezing Jed's hand, she stood up and moved around.

Lindsey knew some about her parents. Not a great deal. It had been her wish not to know much about them because if this worked out the way she thought it would, then there wasn't a lot of point in knowing everything. Now as she looked out the window to the street below, she wished that she'd taken the time to read a little about them.

Below her a limo pulled up and a man got out of the front and opened the door to the rear. A man stepped out, and she watched as he straightened his tie before reaching into the car and helping a woman out. She had no idea if they were her parents or not. It was difficult to see him with his face turned away, but the woman she did know. It was just like that. Her memories of her parents came flooding back.

Her father playing a game of checkers with her. Mom standing in line with her to see a movie. Christmases with them in the big house on the hill, and her grandmother. Lindsey told them that they were here, and Jed came to stand beside her as the car pulled away and the couple stood there holding each other.

"I think I remember them. And when I was taken." Jed nodded but said nothing to her. "I was almost eight. There was a man…two men that came to get me. I was supposed to have eaten this snack, but I wasn't allowed to have any, so I didn't eat it. When he came into my room, Dean Landon, I was sitting at my table coloring. He had a brother, his name was…Willie. They told me that I was going for a ride to my grandmother's house, and I remember thinking that wasn't right."

"Did your grandmother…was she at the house?" Lindsey had to think. When she nodded, Jed did as well. "We all thought so. Did you see her that night?"

"Sort of. She was standing at the bottom of the stairs when I was brought down. Dean had me over his shoulder, and Willie was telling me to keep quiet, that Grandmother mustn't know that I was awake. I was afraid of her, you see." While they spoke quietly, a second car pulled up, this one a regular taxi. As the woman got out of the back, Lindsey saw her grandmother. "She was there. I think…I think she knew I was being taken away."

"Don't say anything just yet. We had a feeling that she might be in on it. Asher did anyway. He knows her, you see. It's why we never gave their attorney too much information. We didn't want her to run before this came to light." Jed pulled her closer to him and held her as he whispered in her ear. "She killed Dean a few years after you were taken. His brother Willie died a few weeks ago, and his estate had an envelope in it that went to our attorney. It was to go to whoever asked about you, as Lindsey Decker."

The door opened while she was still trying to wrap her mind around what he'd just told her. The fact that they'd known before this wasn't what bothered her, but that her own grandmother could do this to her. Her dad walked in the door and Lindsey looked at him. Moving toward him, Jed close beside her, she put out her hand to shake his.

"Dad?"

He pulled her to him. Her father was a big man, not fat but tall and stout, and his hug nearly took her breath away. As he held her, sobbing about how he'd missed her, her mom came to touch her, her fingers dancing over her face, then her arms, as she, too, cried how much she'd missed her.

She had no idea what they were saying. It was mostly about missing her, and they had never given up hope. Lindsey was overwhelmed, and when a hand touched her on the back, she stepped back to him. Jed was there, and she knew that Zak was close too.

They'd already talked about how they would handle her having two mates. Zak would be close, but it would be Jed she was married to. It would set well, she'd been told, and that they couldn't know that Zak or the rest of them were not human. It frightened her to think that there was someone out there looking for her and dragons, and she agreed readily to this plan.

"Mom? Dad? This is my husband, Jed Benson. Jed, these are my parents, Gabby and Donald Cartwright." She introduced them to Jed's brothers, and wished now that the rest of them could have met them as well. They were there, of course, but Zak was the only one she could pull from his host so far from the house and the magic there.

Then she introduced them to Jacob and Elbert. "This is their grandda and father. They're here for moral support."

The door opened again and there she stood. Lindsey had never understood her grandmother, and now she knew why she'd never liked her. It had been a hate-hate relationship since she'd been a child. And now that she remembered everything, it was hard for her not to walk up to her grandmother and ask her why she'd done this.

"Gabriella. I see you managed to scare everyone needlessly." Lindsey told her that she preferred to be called by the name she'd lived with for the last twenty years. "And I do not wish to call you such a common name. You are Gabriella Cartwright. And that is all you will ever be to me."

"All right, but it's not even Cartwright now. It's Benson." Her grandmother looked around the room and paled when she saw Asher. "I see that you've met some of my family. Jed, this is my grandmother, the one I was telling you about."

Lindsey wasn't sure if she got the dig or not, but her grandmother had to have a seat as well as a drink of water. It surprised her to see neither her mother nor father go to her aid, but instead seemed to distance themselves from her even more. Lindsey might have thought it funny had she not been so pissed off about her.

As if queued, the doors opened again and several of the wait staff came in to take their orders. Lindsey was seated between her parents, her grandmother at the end of the table, and Asher at the head. Jed and Zak sat across from her, and she looked at Jed now when asked what she wanted to order. Thankfully, Jed came to her rescue and ordered for her.

"So what have you been up to? I mean, we know that you've been married only a short time. How did you two meet?" Glancing at Jed, she had no idea how to answer her mom. She didn't think telling her that she'd been doing nothing but trying to stay one step ahead of jail was a good thing. But she had to tell them something. Jed and Zak had told her to tell them what she was comfortable with. She supposed the truth was going to have to do.

"I've been mostly trying to keep out of trouble." That made them laugh, and she shook her head. "No, I've seriously been trying to keep out of jail, and it's been hard. Most of the time…for a long time I didn't have anywhere to live. And more often than not, I was homeless."

"No." Her mom looked at her dad as she continued. "We tried to find you. We've never…every year on the anniversary of your disappearance, we'd renew the drive to find you. There was…I have no idea what happened that night. We woke in a fog and it wasn't until the maid told us you were gone that we realized something had happened to all of us. Not like you, of course, but we were drugged."

"I wasn't." Jed nodded at her when she looked at him. "In fact, until recently, like only minutes before you came in the room, I had no memory of what had happened that night either. But it came back to me when I saw you."

Her grandmother dropped her fork, and wine spilled on the table when she tried to stand up. The waiter next to her stopped her by putting a hand on her shoulder. When Lindsey looked at Asher, he told her to go on.

"There was a man, Dean Landon, who came into my room that night. He was surprised to find me awake. I had been given a snack that night that I hadn't eaten. I wasn't allowed to have things like cookies and cakes at bedtime."

Her dad looked at her, then to the end of the table as she continued. "He told me that I had to be quiet, that if she found out I was awake there would be hell to pay. He also told me that if I screamed or made any kind of noise, the rest of his crew would kill my parents by cutting their throats. I never really understood why she hated me so much, but I guess even then I was afraid of her."

"She's confused is all." Her grandmother tried to stand again, but the man held her there. "Unhand me, you fool. I'm not going to stand for you touching me this way. Donald, tell him to release me. I've a terrible headache and I need to go and rest."

"Gabrielle, could you…Lindsey, could you finish your story, please? I think I'd very much like to hear it all." Her father never looked at her as he spoke, but kept his eyes on his mother. "Mother, if you move from the seat, you'll regret it for the rest of your days."

"I was told that I'd be safe. That I'd never have to be beaten again. I'd never been hit, but I was afraid of what he meant by 'grandmother.' That was when I saw her. She was waiting at the door for us." As she watched her grandmother struggle with the man, Lindsey turned to the men in her life that meant the world to her and always would. "When we got to the car—it was a dark van, really—Willie told me to lay down really quietly and that everything would be all right. I did as he said because I could see Grandmother standing there with her cane. As we drove away, they handed me a burger and I pretended to eat it as they talked in the front of the van."

"You knew the men?" She told her mother that she hadn't, but they'd told her who they were. "And this burger, you didn't eat it? They knew that?"

"No, but when I lay down I could hear them talking. They were supposed to drop me off, you see. Take me to a part of town where there were…I remember thinking at the time that I had no idea what an undesirable was. But that was where I was to go. As I lay there I must have fallen asleep, because when I woke up the next time I was in the home, in a small bed that smelled."

"Lindsey, honey. Was it your grandmother? Are you sure about that?" She nodded at her dad and looked down the table at her. "Those men, did you ever see them again?"

"Oh, yes. Landon came to the home where I was sometimes and made sure that I had more than the rest. He was caring for me, I suppose, in his own way."

"Millicent Cartwright…." The man holding her grandmother down finally spoke. "You are under arrest for the kidnapping of Gabriella Cartwright, the murder of Dean Landon, and the—"

Her grandmother stood and slapped the man. As he stumbled away from her, she lunged at Lindsey and her parents. Before she could even get close enough to touch her, Jed had taken her down and Zak was standing there holding Lindsey. It was over that quickly.

Chapter 12

Gabby watched her daughter. She had no idea what she'd been doing with her life. The only information that they'd been given before coming here today was that she'd been found and that she was married. And Gabby really liked the family that she had married into.

"What will happen to her? I mean, will she go to jail?" Gabby smiled. Even after all that her grandmother had done to her, she was still concerned. "I don't really care, mind you. But I'd hate to have her out seeking revenge on us."

Gabby burst out laughing. "And here I was thinking after all she'd done to you, you were still sorry for her. Don't be, even if you were going to be. She's a nasty old woman, and I hope that she gets everything she deserves." Gabby found herself admiring her daughter, something that she'd never thought she'd do. "I know nothing about you…what you've been doing, how you survived all this time. I know that you were in that horrid home, but nothing else."

Gabby had also found out from Asher's attorney that she'd been imprisoned, and he'd warned her, quite firmly, that if she had a problem with it then there was the door. She liked him as well.

"I'm happy now. That's all that should matter. And you're here." Gabriella...Lindsey looked around the room and looked at the two men that could not take their eyes off her. They were in love, the three of them. It didn't take a lot to see that. "You should know that I'm married to them both if you're going to be around. I'd like for you to know them, but if that's something that you don't approve of, then I'm not going to tell you I'll fix it. I'm in love with them both."

"They're not human." Lindsey looked at her. "I'm not that dense. I don't know what they are, but I'm assuming that they're your...mates, I think they're called." Lindsey told her that they were. "I'm not sure how I feel about you having two men in your life, but it seems to work for the three of you. Asher and his wife, they have another male in their life too?"

"Yes. His name is Kiaran. They're dragons." Gabby felt her heart take a hard tumble. Dragons. "Not all of them are dragons. Just the...I guess you could call them the human part of them. Zak can change to his human here because of what I am. The other dragons are a part of the men you see here. Each of them have one that they can call to. And they're old too. Extremely old."

"I see." She didn't, but Gabby was trying. "And what is it that you are? I'm assuming that you're like them...a dragon?"

"No. I can talk to them. Call them if I need them, or as is happening now, I'm a beacon for them to come to the land that is protected by magic and will keep them safe." Gabby found her head bobbing as if she understood, but all she could think was her daughter was off her rocker. Not really, but it was difficult to take in. "Mom?"

"No more, please. I'm working through this right now." Lindsey nodded and sat still while Gabby felt her mind roll in circles. "Tell me about your life before the men. I mean, what did you do?"

"I was a housekeeper for a man that had me chained to the floor for over a year. His plan was to kill me when I'd worn out my welcome, then put my things in a box on the wall near where the other women's things were put. But he's dead now; a dragon killed him by chopping him in—" Gabby said her name and Lindsey smiled. "I wanted you to get it all at once. That way when you go home and leave me, you'll have something to think about."

"Scaring me off, are you?" Lindsey only shrugged. "I'd rather not go just yet. I'm very…overwhelmed doesn't even begin to cover what I'm feeling right now, but I'd like to get to know you again. This woman that you've become, I don't know her at all."

"I don't know you either. I mean, I know who you are, but nothing more. And to be honest, I'm not sure what to do with you in my life now. Do you?" Gabby had no idea either. It was as if they were strangers. Mother and daughter, but strangers all the same.

"We can work on being friends. I'd like to have you around so I can…I don't think shopping is something that you do, is it?"

"No. I have a house that is…it's huge compared to what I have lived in. And while it's furnished for the most part, there are things we still need." She grinned, the first true one that Gabby had seen as yet. "I have a garden. And a tractor. I'm not sure what to do with either of them, but I'm excited. And Jed said I could try raising chickens if

I wanted. Essie has her herbs and we'll go mushroom hunting in the spring, but I'm excited to have things of my own."

Gabby didn't say that there were things at their house that were hers. And after they were both gone, it would all be hers. Now that Gabby thought of it, preserving a room for this long, hoping for the child to return, had been just silly. And stupid. She looked away when she felt her heart twist up in how long it had been.

"Mom? I'm not going to leave you if you don't want me to." Gabby nodded, then shook her head. "Tell me what you're thinking. Maybe we can fix it."

"Your room. It's just the way you left it. All your school books are still on your desk. The bed is made, of course, but it's all pink and flowers. I guess I never thought of you as a grown woman. I still…I have no idea what I was thinking, but you're not going to want any of those things." Lindsey pulled her hand to her cheek and held it there as Gabby thought of all she'd missed. "I have missed you so much, Lindsey."

"Is Mr. Sham there?" It took Gabby several seconds to remember who that was. The teddy bear…the one that she'd gotten for her when she and Donald were on a business trip when Gabby had been pregnant with her little girl. "I'd like to have him if he's there. And Miss Bear."

"The skunk. You were the only child I knew that would name your stuffed animals the most ridiculous names." Lindsey grinned again. "I have them all. The housekeeping staff goes in and dusts every week, and I think one of them finally convinced me to take all your clothing out of the drawers and closet, but I doubt you could have worn them anyway."

"I'm pretty sure I've gotten taller." Gabby nodded, still crying about all that she'd lost. "Mom, please don't cry for missing me. We want to have babies, Jed, Zak, and I, and we'd very much like for you to spoil them rotten. You can make up for missing me by being in their lives. Too much if you want."

"I'd very much like that." Gabby looked over at Donald, who had been talking with the police. Millicent was gone, but her shrill voice was still echoing in her head. She was actually upset that they thought her involvement in the kidnapping of their daughter should get her into trouble.

"I've talked to the attorney. I can tell you what happened if you'd like to know." Gabby looked at Lindsey and nodded. "She hired Landon to take me and he brought his brother along to help. When Willie, Landon's brother, couldn't find his brother after he'd gone to see Millicent to get his reward for taking me away, he figured she'd killed him. So instead of going to the police, because he had no proof and wasn't really an upstanding sort of guy, he kept track of things and me over the years so that when he died or someone came looking for me, they'd know."

"I'm guessing that whatever he had on her, it was a lot." Lindsey told her mom it was the code to the house alarm and the instructions on which room that they could find her in. "I wonder why he didn't come to us. I mean, we would have gotten you back and this nightmare would have been over with."

"She told them that you two were drunks and that I was being abused terribly." She didn't tell her mom all of it. There was no reason for her to ever know that not only had the two men gone to see them sprawled out on the couch after the drugs, but that one of them had taken pictures of them and Willie had developed them.

Her mom looked at her dad, and she did too. Jed was talking to him now, and he looked broken. Lindsey knew that her dad and grandmother had never gotten along, but this would be something horrific to take in. His own mother had taken her only grandchild and given her away.

"Did she plan to kill you, do you think?" Lindsey looked at her mom, who was still staring at her dad. "Millicent, do you suppose it was in her plan to kill you?"

"She thought they had." Her mom nodded and stood up to go to her husband. Zak sat beside her and took her hand into his warmer one. He asked her how she was holding up. "Okay. I told her about us. All of us."

"She's trustworthy." It wasn't a question, but she nodded to him all the same. "I've spoken to Jed, and we were wondering if you'd like for them to come and stay with us a few days. Not in the house with us, but close. Asher said that he could put something together for them."

"I'd like that, but he doesn't have to go to that much trouble. I think they're just as happy in a hotel for now. I'm not sure…we really don't know each other." Zak held her hand and told her he loved her. "And I love you. But I was wondering if I will ever have something normal in my life. I've been kidnapped, chained up, in jail, and nearly shot. It would be nice to not have so much going on, don't you think?"

After dinner was started again and the wait staff left them, it was much more relaxed. No one mentioned Millicent, nor did anyone comment on the fact that now she was sitting with Jed on one side and Zak on the other.

They were her men, and her parents were going to have to get used to it.

~~~

The drive back to the house was made in silence. Jed was a little worried about Lindsey, but she'd told them several times that she was just fine. He knew that today had taken a great deal out of her, and there was the thing tomorrow that they were going to have to deal with as well. The bodies at the other property had been found in the cave not far from where Cox had lived.

"She's asleep." He glanced over at Zak when he spoke quietly. "I have to tell you something. But I don't want you to freak out."

"I do not freak out. I'm an old man who has seen a great deal, and have lived through more than my share of—"

"Lindsey is pregnant." Jed nearly took them to the median. "Yeah, you don't freak out, do you?"

"How do you know?" When Zak cocked a brow at him, he nearly snarled at him. "You know that she is, so the least you can do is share with me how you know. I'm sure she doesn't."

"No. She doesn't. But she will soon enough. I'd say she's not far along, about two weeks." Zak turned in his seat to look at Lindsey as she slept in the back seat. "She's going to be a wonderful mother. And the reason I know that she's breeding is because I can smell it on her. I had no idea what I was smelling to be honest, but I asked Elbert. He told me."

Jed continued to drive, trying to think what he was to do now. Tell her? Not tell her? She'd want to know, he was sure, but when did women want this kind of information? He glanced at Zak when he laughed.
~~~

"How long have you known? And for the record, this is sort of scaring the shit out of me." He told him it was scaring him too. "Do you know what she's having?"

"I don't. But I do know that it's like the three of us. Magical and some dragon in it. I'm not sure how much, but I can feel it calling to me." Zak looked at him. "Do you think she'll be okay with that?"

"I think she'll be thrilled to death with a baby." He knew what Zak was asking him, and tried to think about how she'd feel with having such a mix of a baby. "I think that if it had four heads and three legs, she'd love it. I'm still…pregnant. Wow, that's great. We're going to be fathers."

"So you know, Essie is breeding too. I don't know if they are aware of it yet, but I'm sure that Kiaran is. So when they tell us, we need to act surprised." Jed nodded. Two babies coming into the world. Their family was growing. "Jed, do you think this will change things for us? With her, I mean?"

"I don't know why it would." He looked in the rearview mirror, adjusting it so that he could see her. "She's been through a great deal and she still loves us. I think that says a lot, don't you?"

"Are you two finished?" Jed should have known that she was listening to them. "I'm not sure what you think will change, and having a baby will be a lot of work. But I know for a fact that the two of you will be wonderful fathers, as well as caregivers. Not to mention, the entire family helping us raise them."

She sat up and put her hand on her belly. Jed pulled to the side of the road and then off the highway all together. They were close to home, perhaps another ten minutes, but he needed to hold her now. And he was sure that she could use a hug as well. Getting out, she exited the car too and stood near him and Zak. The three of them held onto each other tightly for several minutes.

"I want you." Jed rubbed his hand down to her ass and pulled her tightly against him even as Zak held onto her breast. "Christ, I need to fuck you."

As they took her deeper in the woods, all he could think about was being inside of her, taking her right there in the wooded area. When they found an old picnic table, he took off his shirt and laid it over it. She was naked when she lay over it, her legs spread open for them.

Moving between her legs, Jed fisted his cock. His clothing, like hers and Zak's, had disappeared almost as soon as they were out there. Zak moved to the seat at the table and began suckling at her breasts even as Jed entered her slowly.

She was wet and tight, her body slipping over his cock noisily as he pulled her legs up to his shoulders. Taking her slowly, he watched Zak as he stood up and fucked her breasts as Lindsey held his cock in her fingers. When she pulled him to her mouth and Zak moaned, Jed felt his balls tighten up as they filled. He loved watching the two of them together.

He let her legs go, and Jed moaned as she wrapped them around his hips. Pulling back enough so that she released him, Jed dropped to his knees and pulled her to the edge of the table. This was what he wanted. To drink from her when she came sucking Zak's cock.

He ate her hungrily. She tasted hot, wet, and spicy. Every time she came, her cum filling his mouth, he wanted more. Needed more of her. And when he slid his fingers into her ass, she came screaming out his name as Zak emptied himself all over her face and breasts. Then she stood up, and he nearly begged her to take him in her mouth when she told him to lift her. He was buried inside of her again, and he started to lay her over the table when she told Zak to come to her back.

"Fuck me this way." Her body was no longer wrapped around him, but her legs were spread. Zak moved up behind her and when she told him to take her, he looked up at him. There was no way she wanted them both to fuck her. "Please. I'm dying to have you both in me at the same time. Fuck me, Zak. Please, take me."

It took some doing. She was shorter than both of them, and Jed ended up holding her around his waist while Zak moved to take her tight cherry. As he moved slowly, his cock filling her, Jed could feel the sweat rolling down his back in an effort not to come too soon. As soon as Zak was buried deep within her she looked up at him.

Putting her on the ground again, he was careful not to hurt her. Christ, if she moaned or even groaned just a little, he was finished. And when he pulled back as Zak moved forward, he had to take several deep breaths before he was able to move again.

"Christ, this is wonderful. Fuck me please. Make me come this way." Jed watched her face for any sign of pain, but the harder Zak fucked her from behind, the harder her pussy hit his groin. He held her hips to steady her as Zak pulled hard at her breasts. When he looked at his cock as it moved in and out of her body, Jed threw back his head and came, his entire body feeling the release as if it were his first time.

Zak came too, his dragon moving over his body as if he wanted to shift. When she screamed out her own release, Jed came again, this time feeling the world shift under his feet and his heart nearly explode. Stars danced behind his lids as he held her to him and bit deeply into her shoulder, bringing her again as she went limp in his arms.

Jed couldn't move. Not that he was in any kind of hurry right now, but he was sure that she was cold. Lifting his head, he looked into Zak's eyes and knew just what he was feeling. This woman was the best thing that had ever happened to them. Bar none.

"I love you, Jed. I think I always have, but I really do love you." Jed nodded, too overwhelmed with emotion to do much more than that. His eyes were filled with tears, blurring his vision as he told Zak that he loved him as well. Zak backed from her, his cock still semi-hard, and lifted Lindsey into his arms while he dressed. Jed was shaking a little, his body weak from the most amazing climax. When Zak handed him Lindsey, he sat down on the table and held her while Zak dressed too.

They didn't say anything on the way home. He drove slowly, his body sated for now, and thought of what they had done tonight. It was going to make their bedroom more fun, he thought, and looked over at Zak when he laughed.

"She's never going to be boring, is she?" Jed said he didn't think so. "And our children, do you suppose they'll be just like her?"

"Yes. More so, I'm betting." He thought about it. "I hope they are just like her. She's all I ever wanted in a mate and more."

"Yeah, me too." As Zak sat there, the same goofy grin on his face that he was sure what was on his, Jed laughed again. "What is it?"

"Tomorrow. I was worried about her going to talk to the police about what she'd found at the house and what she'd done while there. But now, I'm sure she can handle about anything."

Tomorrow would be hard on her, but Jed was pretty sure that she could handle it. He knew that he felt better about it already. As they pulled in front of their home, he lifted her out of the back seat and carried her inside. The bed was big enough for the three of them, but both he and Zak moved out of the room at the same time to go to the deck surrounding the house. Daisy was waiting for them on the railing.

"Master, there are more dragons coming." Jed nodded. Lindsey had already told him that she had felt them. "One is sick and will need attention when he arrives. The female, his sister, is not well either, but she is stronger than him."

"Does Asher know?" She said that she'd told him before coming here. "Good. I have a favor to ask of you. And you may turn me down should you wish. But know that I have cleared it with your king. I would like for you to stay with Lindsey at all times. I know that you'll have other work to do. I'm not sure what that would be, but I'd very much like for you to be her helper."

"Me, my lord? You wish for me to care for your mate?" She bowed low before him, her small wings spread out so that she was nearly flat with it. "It will be my greatest honor, my lord. To watch over the one that will keep us safe."

"You honor us with your help." Zak nodded at her as well when she looked at him. "Daisy, she's breeding, did you know that?"

"We all do, my lord. She will have a great son, and he will gather us all together and keep us safe. The king and his child will rule with a firm but fair hand, and we will be united again, as a great family."

After she left them, Jed looked out over the trees and mountains. It was going to be a good life from now on, for all of them. He grinned when he thought of what his dad would say when he found out about the children coming.

Chapter 13

The pair of dragons arrived just before the sun came up. The brother, Dawod, was indeed very ill. He'd been shot by something iron, and the poison was running through his body through his blood. As he lay there resting, Elbert tended to his sister, Ada. She, he knew, was going to be a handful.

As Lindsey translated what the dragon wanted, he could see the sparkle in her eye. Lindsey was going to hit the big dragon if the being kept up with her demands. "She said that he will need wart berry root. Do you know what that is? There was some in a field about a mile or so back, she's telling me."

"There is some drying in the barn that we can start with. I've already made a poultice with some of it for his wounds. And a tea for his belly." Elbert glanced at the dragon before talking to Lindsey again. "You can take her should you like."

"I'm going to hurt her if she doesn't stop barking orders at me. Doesn't she see that we're doing the best we can?" When Lindsey turned to the dragon, he could almost understand what she was saying but not enough to help. It had been too many years since he'd heard the language spoken, and more so since he'd said any of the words.

As Lindsey sent the now healed Salomon on his way to gather what he could, Elbert poured the mixture over the wounds that were deep and hot with fever. He looked at Lindsey when she said his name. She asked him if he was going to make it.

"I don't know. He's very ill and coming here has weakened him a great deal. Perhaps in a few days, after much rest, I'll have a better answer for you." Dawod moved his wings for him when he moved closer to put more of the herbs on him. "Do you know what has touched him? What iron will do to a dragon? Any dragon?"

"I read in the book you gave me that it's the same as giving them poison. What I don't understand, and maybe we'll figure this out, is why someone would shoot him with it. I mean, what harm has he done to them, this hunter of dragons?" As she moved to help him with Ada's wounds, he thought of how to answer her when she continued. "There are things in that book that scare me, Elbert. Did you know that every part of the dragon's body, even their blood, is magical? I mean, I guess in a way I knew that, but I can see why someone would hunt them now. But they're so…wonderfully beautiful. They're majestic and wholly without compare to anything we've ever seen in this century. Why kill them?"

He wondered as well. At one time, when he'd been but a child, the skies were filled with the big creatures. Some of them were smaller than even Daisy, who now sat upon Lindsey's shoulder.

He wondered, as did Jacob, if this would mean they'd have to take more care with the animals that roamed in the woods surrounding the land. A dragon could eat its weight in meat daily, and this dragon they were helping weighed at least fifty stone. With the combined amount of them that were here now, the deer and other animals would not last a season. He decided to talk to Asher about it.

The dragon Dawod was getting worse. Even as he moved to help Elbert tend to his wounds, he was dying. He looked at his sister and knew that she could see it too. When her body stiffened and she stood up, Lindsey wrapped her arms around her great body and held her. The big dragon nudged her shoulder, and when Lindsey stepped away from her, she took to the skies.

"She wants us to make him comfortable." Elbert nodded. "She said she was sorry for her temper, but that she had known for several days now that he wasn't going to make it. He took the iron meant for her."

When it was time, Dawod nodded at him, his eyes burning with fever and pain. Elbert wanted to end his suffering now but knew that he could not. The dragon was as much a part of his magic as any of the other animals that roamed the area. Shifting to his great dog, he watched as the dragon took his last breaths, knowing what was going to come next…as had his sister.

Dawod raised his hand and put it gently on Lindsey. He could have easily crushed her, but he only pushed her to a sitting position as he sat up a little to look into her eyes. It cost him a great deal, his body already weak with the poison, and he moved slowly as he captured her fully with his magic. Lindsey and her mates were about to get something profound, and Elbert was glad to have been there to see it.

His magic, all of what he was and who he was, shifted from him to her. Ada had known that she could have taken it; the magic of her brother would have rightly come to her. But she'd forfeited it for Lindsey, the woman who would help more than just the two of them. As his magic left his body, the part of him that made him dragon, his beautiful but damaged wings, rose up from his body and moved to Lindsey. As they wrapped around her, Dawod's magic was spent. As he disappeared, his body no longer his, small faerie dust sprinkled to the earth and flowers bloomed brighter and stronger where his body had been. A reminder to all that came to this area that a great loss was felt this day.

A great cry from the mountains was heard. The ground trembled from the pain of Ada's loss. As trees swayed in the morning sun, the dragon brothers of Eve and Anthony came to the clearing, as did Silco, his mate, and their child. Even Salomon, far away on a job, returned to pay homage to one of their fallen. Jacob and his own sons, strong and respective, stayed back, their heads bowed low as they dropped to one knee. Dawod had not been in their lives long. Some did not even know him, but they did respect that there had been a great loss.

Lindsey was picked up a few minutes later. She was fine, she told Zak as he carried her to the porch. And for all outward appearances, she looked no different than she had before. But he knew, as did the others, that Lindsey had been given a great gift, greater than any before her had been given. She was given the magic of a powerful and very old dragon. Elbert shifted back to his human and watched her carefully after giving her a large glass of fresh juice.

"What happened?" No one answered her question, and she looked at him. "You were there, Elbert. What happened? I know that he died, but after that, I'm not sure."

"He has given himself to you and your mates." Lindsey asked him what that meant. "You are more dragon than human now. I do not know if you will be able to shift, but you can fly with them. They will no longer just speak to you here, but over long distances as well. The man who killed Dawod, you will know him on sight. His blood now is a part of yours so that you can protect all that come here. Asher and Essie are their king and queen, but you are their savior more than ever. You are now, all of you, Dragon Saviors."

Jacob bowed when Elbert did, then the others. He could see from the corner of his eye that the other dragons, too, were paying their respect. The men and women that lived here, now and in the future, would be cared for and protected above even themselves. The dragons would be safe here now and forever.

"I did nothing that you didn't do to help them." Lindsey was embarrassed, everyone could see that, but Elbert nodded at her and said nothing. "Were you given this thing? This gift?"

"Nay, I am not worthy of it." He hadn't meant to make her upset, but she stood up so quickly that he backed away, his dog whimpering within him. "I did not mean that the way that you seem to think. I am not the one that was chosen by the former queen. I do not have it in me…I have more power now than I can use, more than I have ever needed to survive. But in the coming years, decades and decades from now, the dragons will need you more than ever. Protecting them, healing them as you tried to do with Dawod, was...you did this without thought to your own safety. Nay, you did this because you were the only one that could. The rest, the family, has received some of what you have been gifted, but you have it all. All of the dragon's magic."

She sat on the chair for the rest of the afternoon. When, at lunchtime or thereafter, the police showed up, Lindsey told them all that she knew and then walked with them to the house that had been her prison. Elbert did not go with her, but sent Jacob along with Zak and Jed. Elbert had things to do, and they would not get done with him taking a stroll with the police.

Essie joined him in the house a bit later. "She will do fine, won't she, Elbert? I have come to love her like a sister, and I don't want anything to happen to her."

"She is like you, my lady. An immortal." Essie told him that wasn't what she meant. "You mean this thing with the police? She has made her peace with the man that harmed her. And he is no longer here to remind her of what had happened. Lady Lindsey will be better when this is over, yes, but she is well now."

"Did you know that we're to have a child? Lindsey and I are both pregnant?" He said that he did, as did most of the house. "I'm worried about that too. I don't know if I can be a mother, or a very good one anyway."

"You will be the best. The two of you, Lady Lindsey and you, will raise your children with your hearts, not what your parents or lack of them have taught you. Great children, both men and women, will come to this family now, and more as the others gain their mates as well. We will have much to celebrate in the coming months." He handed her a glass of the juice he'd given to Lindsey, and smiled when she drank it down quickly. "You will need to drink more, my child. You will need a great deal of rest as well. Having a dragon child will take a great deal out of you."

"I will." After a little more conversation, she left him to his work. Caroline appeared in his kitchen just after two, and he told her what he'd witnessed. He was still smiling about it when she shook her head at him.

"You are an old softy. Do the men know that?" He said nothing, not wanting to give her any kind of thought to tease him more. "I have come to tell you that the other dragons are coming. Not as many as we had thought, but a few more. You should also know that the earth has agreed to help out with the meat and other items that you will need. All the animals, all of them, are breeding now and will continue to do so until things are evened out. And we have called in more to…it feels a bit odd to do this, as if we are bringing them here to die, but the earth is so happy to have their dragons back that they're willing to help at most anything."

"Have you seen the faerie circle that Dawod has left here?" She told him that she had. "It is a glorious thing, to see that again. Not that I wish them to die, but to see the magic to return to this realm again. We will have to celebrate come harvest time. I've even noticed that the trees and fruits are heavy with their bounty too. I will begin to make ways to preserve as much as I can of that as well."

Elbert thought that Caroline should stay a while and she said she'd think on it. Abraham was not doing well in his studies to become more in with the century, so she'd sent him to her sister. He would, Caroline said, do much better with her. As they began preparations for dinner, the family returned home to say that the police were going to begin looking for Cox. And the women. It would be a long hard winter on them, but Elbert knew that they'd have to look beyond the yard of Cox and to the caves.

~~~

Ralph Sharp moved along the path that he'd been walking for several days now without making a sound. He was as silent as the woods around him and knew that he was close to the thing he was tracking.

Three days ago he'd seen his first big one…well, two of them actually. And he'd actually gotten off several shots with his big guns before they'd disappeared behind a mountain. He knew that he'd hit the bigger of the two of them, but now the sucker was gone. Dragons were going to give him everything, just as soon as he could prove to the world that they were actually out there. There were too many skeptics in the world as far as he was concerned.

About ten years ago, he'd been out with some hunting buddies. Seldom did they actually bag anything but a few hangovers and some unexplained cuts and bruises. But every year they'd get together by telling their families that they were going hunting and disappear for about two weeks. Sometimes longer, but seldom any less than that.

They'd been really drunk, he would admit that now, but they saw a big dark shape under the water where they'd been staying. It moved like a fucking torpedo and they'd watched it from the top decking of their cabin. But when the others went in the house as the rain got to be too much, the big thing stuck its head out of the water and stared at him. Even from across the deep lake, he knew it had been huge. And when the thing rose up out of the water and took off to the skies, it had taken him the rest of
~~~

the trip to convince himself and his buddies that he'd actually seen a dragon. Now they avoided him, telling him that he was off his rocker. Ralph didn't care; he was after bigger game and he'd not touched a drop of liquor since.

He'd done a lot of research on the thing he'd seen. Honestly, he had thought he was nuts as well, until someone had come to him to tell him that he was on the right track, and she had given him a thick book on dragons. Ralph had read it cover to cover so many times that he was sure that he could recite each line of it without turning to the page. And it had been very helpful as well. The woman, Helena, had told him she'd be back to help him when the time was right. That had been so long ago he figured she had forgotten him.

But he'd not forgotten her or the dragons. And lately, he had seen five more, all of them heading in the same direction…somewhere in Ohio. Once they were there it was as if they simply disappeared. But Ralph knew that they were out there now, and he was going to find one.

The book had told him their worth. After much research on what some of the old words in the book meant, he discovered the dragons were purely magic, and that if he were to get one alive, he would be set for the rest of his life. Their tears alone could make him very wealthy. Then there were the other parts of them.

A dragon scale could be used for many things. Cures for one, but they could make a woman have a child with nothing more than a touch of one. The eyes of a dragon, if cooked properly, would make the person who drank the tea from them see the future of not just himself, but whoever he touched as well.

The blood of a dragon could make one live forever, cure any disease, as well as enrich the earth that it fell upon. Ralph had no such plans for the blood of one of these creatures to ever touch the earth. He had a great many plans for every drop of it. He would, in a word, be rich.

The sound behind him made him pause. Hiding behind a tree was difficult with all his equipment, but he was still and quiet as the woman walked into the sunlight. Ralph could not believe the beautiful thing before him.

She was tall, taller than his own six foot frame, but tiny in stature. She had white blonde hair that hung well below her hips, and her eyes, even from the distance between he and her, seemed to be clear blue…like ice, he thought. When she stood still too, looking in his direction, Ralph had the urge not just to run but to run screaming from her. He stood perfectly still, not even breathing hard in the event that she'd see him. But for some reason, Ralph thought she knew just where he was.

A swarm of butterflies—not really the name for a group of them, but it was all he could think of as they hit him—pelted him with their wings as they seemed to come out of nowhere. He moved then, flapping his hands, trying his best to keep them out of his mouth and eyes. The woman laughed then, the sound coming across the distance making him think that she'd done this to him, conjured them up so that they'd attack. When he was fully exposed, the butterflies—a kaleidoscope, he just remembered them being called—disappeared into the tops of the trees.

"So you are the dragon killer." He'd killed one? This was news to him, but before he could ask her where the body was, she continued. "I'm to visit the king and queen now. What do you think they'll do should they find out that you are killing their dragons?"

"Reward me?" He doubled over in pain. It felt as if he'd had his belly split open. But when he looked, there was nothing there, not even a wrinkle in his shirt. "What the fuck are you?"

"A witch." He glanced up at her to see if she was kidding or not. "I'm neither white nor black…something in between, I guess. You, however, are all black: your heart is not good at all."

"No one is either black or white. There is some gray in all of us." Her laughter again made him flinch from the expected attack of butterflies. "What do you care if I kill myself a dragon? It's not like they should be around here anymore. Hell, until a while back, I didn't even know that they were real."

"That's what they were hoping for." She moved closer and he was lifted up. Not by his legs and body, but by something else. "You are not going to be happy, nor will you live all that long, if you keep on this path. The saviors will kill you."

She'd not said they might, but that they would. And for some reason, the threat of it scared him a great deal. As he was lowered to the ground, he stood this time. He watched as she moved around him, unable to turn and look at her as she was at his back.

"You said that I was a murderer. Did I actually kill a dragon?" He tried not to sound so excited, but he was. To have killed a great beast all on his own. When she didn't answer him, he tried to look behind him, but she wasn't there. When he turned again, she was nearly at his face, right in front of him. "Are you using some kind of mind control on me?"

"You don't have enough sense to get out of the woods. Me trying to control you would be pointless. And time consuming. I don't want to mess with you anyway." He started to tell her not to talk to him that way, but she only laughed at him again. "You are the biggest moron I've ever met, and believe me, I've met quite a few in my lifetime."

He thought her to be only about twenty-five, if that much, but he had a feeling she was much older, even older than him. As she sat on the ground, her legs as bare as her feet, she leaned back on her palms and looked at him. Ralph felt the urge to run again.

"You killed a friend of mine. He was old and revered as a dragon. He and I had a wonderful life as friends and you killed him. Or at least you delivered the blow that eventually ended his life. Don't you feel badly for me?" He didn't answer her, sensing a trap. "His sister is a good dragon too. Should you have hit her with your iron, you would have messed up the entire lifecycle that is running right now. I, myself, am included in this time frame, yet I find myself reluctant to go and see to it."

He had no idea what she was talking about. And worse than that, he wasn't sure he wanted to know. As he stood there, feeling exposed, he wondered if she was insane when a great bear moved out of the woods toward them. Ralph could not make his body run or his mouth scream out a warning had he been inclined. There she sat, watching the lumbering creature come at them both. When the bear was behind the woman, facing him, she put out her hand and he touched his nose to her fingers before sitting down on the grass beside her. The woman looked up at him as she rubbed the fur behind the bear's ear.

"I am neither insane nor am I very magical. I have some magic, a great deal in some areas, but very little in the way of getting you to stop the nonsense that you're doing right now. I suppose I could kill you, or have bear here do it for me, but like this entire cycle that I was telling you about, you must run your path to cross those of the others or things will not come out in the end. The previous queen told me this." Sighing heavily, she stood up, the bear now on his hind legs and his large long claws extended to him. With a snap of her fingers, the bear dropped to his feet and stood beside her. "You will not stop this, will you? Your insane pursuit of killing the dragons?"

"I already did, according to you. And where is my magic? The book says that I am to get his magic." The pack at his back shifted, and he watched as the book he was talking about was suddenly in her hands. "Hey. That's mine. It was a gift from someone and I want it back."

"Helena the Black gave it to you. She's dead, in the event that you're looking for her to come help you." The pages turned in the book as the woman stood there looking at it. "You have read this, all of it, even the magical pages?"

"Magical pages?" She showed him pages that he'd not even seen. He started to step toward her and the book, but he stopped when the bear growled. "No, I've never seen those pages before. Give me back my book."

"I think not." When the book snapped closed, it disappeared. The woman turned and headed back the way she'd come, the bear walking alongside her. When she stopped and turned again, he wanted to whimper, but his throat, like his body, was frozen tight. Her appearance made him think of nightmares he'd had as a child of the monster in the closet coming to life. "You will die if you continue on your way."

Then, in a heartbeat, she was gone, as was the bear. Ralph dropped to his knees, then to his belly as his head started to turn and spin. Lying there, thinking of what had just happened, all he could really focus on was that it had to be a dream. That nothing, not the woman or the bear, had been there. As his mind began to wrap around what he was trying to convince himself of, he heard her laugh again. She was as real as he was, it appeared.

Ralph decided to lay there for the rest of the night, convincing himself that he was exhausted and needed to rest. He would, he told himself, deal with this in the morning. Closing his eyes, he tried his best not to hear her laughing again as he willed his body to sleep. This was not real, he told himself over and over.

Before You Go…

HELP AN AUTHOR

write a review

THANK YOU!

Share your voice and help guide other readers to these wonderful books. Even if it's only a line or two your reviews help readers discover the author's books so they can continue creating stories that you'll love. Login to your favorite retailer and leave a review. Thank you.

Kathi Barton, author of the bestselling series Force of Nature, lives in Nashport, Ohio with her husband Paul. In addition to writing full time Kathi likes to spend time with her eight grandkids, three children and three children-in-laws. She writes to relax and have fun.

Her muse, a cross between Jimmy Stewart and Hugh Jackman brings them to life for her readers in a way that has them coming back time and again for more. Her favorite genre is paranormal romance with a great deal of spice. You can visit Kathi on line and drop her an email if you'd like. She loves hearing from her fans. aaronskiss@gmail.com.

Follow Kathi on her blog:
http://kathisbartonauthor.blogspot.com/

www.ingramcontent.com/pod-product-compliance
Lightning Source LLC
Chambersburg PA
CBHW032129170626
46808CB00006B/2157

* 9 7 8 1 6 2 9 8 9 3 5 6 3 *